READING
the BONES
A Peggy Henderson Adventure

READING the BONES

A Peggy Henderson Adventure

Gina McMurchy-Barber

A SANDCASTLE BOOK
A MEMBER OF THE DUNDURN GROUP
TORONTO

Editor: Michael Carroll
Design: Erin Mallory
Printer: Webcom

Library and Archives Canada Cataloguing in Publication

McMurchy-Barber, Gina
    Reading the bones / Gina McMurchy-Barber.

ISBN 978-1-55002-732-7

    1. Coast Salish Indians--Juvenile fiction. I. Title.

PS8625.M86R42 2008   jC813'.6   C2007-905732-2

1   2   3   4   5   12   11   10   09   08

Conseil des Arts   Canada Council
du Canada   for the Arts

ONTARIO ARTS COUNCIL
CONSEIL DES ARTS DE L'ONTARIO

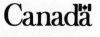
Canadä

We acknowledge the support of **The Canada Council for the Arts** and the **Ontario Arts Council** for our publishing program. We also acknowledge the financial support of the **Government of Canada** through the **Book Publishing Industry Development Program** and **The Association for the Export of Canadian Books**, and the **Government of Ontario** through the **Ontario Book Publishers Tax Credit** program, and the **Ontario Media Development Corporation**.

Care has been taken to trace the ownership of copyright material used in this book. The author and the publisher welcome any information enabling them to rectify any references or credits in subsequent editions.

J. Kirk Howard, President

Printed and bound in Canada.
www.dundurn.com

Dundurn Press
3 Church Street, Suite 500
Toronto, Ontario, Canada
M5E 1M2

Gazelle Book Services Limited
White Cross Mills
High Town, Lancaster, England
LA1 4XS

Dundurn Press
2250 Military Road
Tonawanda, NY
U.S.A. 14150

For Dave, who always urged me to follow my dreams.
And for Aunt Betty, my favourite teacher.

ACKNOWLEDGEMENTS

I would like to thank Victoria Bartlett, a true friend and the Queen of Commas; the Semiahmoo Band for permitting me to learn from their ancestors when I was an archaeology student at Simon Fraser University; Kit Pearson and Mike Mason for their wisdom and encouragement; and my editor, Michael Carroll, for his vision and support.

PROLOGUE

Talusip wipes tears from her face. Her soft skin is creased and ruddy as red cedar bark. Several of the village men lower the body of her husband, Shuksi'em, onto a bed of crushed mussel and clam shells. Now he will lie among his old friends and the young who did not survive.

"Shuksi'em suffered greatly near the end of his life when the sun left the village for many days," whimpers his wife to those near enough to hear. "He never complained, but I know his bones screamed with pain when the rains fell and winds blew. And his back — bent like tall grass heavy with seed — gave him so much trouble he no longer took his daily walks down to the shore to watch the men bring in the salmon. With the days of winter almost upon us, he dreaded what his life would become."

Now that Shuksi'em is dead, though, his crooked old spine makes it easier for the men to place him on his side like a sleeping baby. Talusip puts Shuksi'em's tools beside his curled body. She knows he will need them in the next world. Then she tucks a large piece of fresh smoked salmon near his head and hopes it is enough to tide him over.

The villagers huddle together, backs against a light rain. Some of the women howl with sorrow into the wind. Others whisper in agreement how much the old man will be missed.

"We thank the spirit of Shuksi'em for leaving us many fine storage boxes made from sturdy cedar, each finished

with our family's crest — the Bear," says the clan elder. "And for our giant feast dishes carved from the yew tree. And when the men fish at the river's mouth with his prized bone harpoon points they will send thanks to his spirit."

The young ones remember the times they sat on their mothers' knees listening to the stories Shuksi'em told them. Sometimes his tales were of wisdom or courage. Others, like the one about Quamichan, the flying wild woman who eats children, frightened them so much that they never roam too far from the village.

Talusip recalls the day before death took Shuksi'em how he struggled to finish a wooden ceremonial bowl embraced by the arms and legs of a great frog. It is a gift for her granddaughter's wedding. Talusip's son, Q'am, wants to keep it, but she is afraid of the thing. She has decided to trade the bowl with the Chinook the next time they come to the village.

Taking the large butter clam filled with a paste made of red ochre and fish oil, Talusip begins to spread the mixture over her husband's lifeless body. Her hand trembles and her heart stings. Now she is satisfied that all has been done to prepare her mate for his journey. She steps away and watches the men cover Shuksi'em with a blanket of broken shells, sand, and seaweed in the way her people have done since the Great Spirit created them. Here his body will stay, a short distance from his village, near the shores where he netted fish, close to the forest where he once hunted. Here he will stay forever.

CHAPTER ONE

Just when you think you've got it all figured out, life throws you a curveball. That's what my mom, Elizabeth Henderson, said when my dad died seven years ago. And she said it again when she lost her job last winter after Arrow Communications, an advertising firm, went out of business. When she couldn't find anything close to home, she decided to leave British Columbia and go to Toronto to look for work. Then *zing!* That's when life threw me a curveball and I found out I would have to live with Aunt Margaret and Uncle Stuart until Mom found a job and sent for me. But since then I've learned that sometimes life's curveballs actually work out to be more like — well, let's just say, interesting opportunities. That's what happened one day when I helped Uncle Stuart in the garden.

I had stopped weeding to come and admire the pond hole he was digging when I noticed what looked like a large round stone emerging from the dark, speckled earth. It was smooth and yellowed with age. I bent down and brushed the dirt off with my hand. Then I dug around the sides with my fingers to make it easier to pull out. But as I was about to pry the object loose, my hand flashed my brain an image and I hesitated.

"Hey, Uncle Stu, I think this thing might be a skull." It almost felt silly to say, especially after Uncle Stuart grinned and started stomping around the yard, wailing like some lame ghost. But when he finally stooped closer to peer at the thing in the dirt, I watched the smirk melt from his face.

"Peggy, don't touch it. Get out of there!"

Was he just making more fun of me?

"Go get your aunt right now!"

Okay, maybe not. But now my gaze was mesmerized by the shape in the ground.

"Now, Peggy, now!"

Aunt Margaret and I were back in minutes, standing next to my uncle.

"What do you think it is, Margaret?"

She bent down and examined the object more closely. "My goodness! Is it human?"

Uncle Stuart nervously stroked back his hair. "That's what it looks like to me."

Aunt Margaret's complexion seemed as pasty as uncooked dough. "We'd better call the police, Stuart."

Twenty minutes later the place was swarming with police cars — well, okay, two police cars. But to the dozen or so people gathered across the street from the house, it must have looked like a major crime scene. When Uncle Stuart opened the front door, one of the four men introduced himself.

"Hello, I'm Officer Pratt. I'm a forensics specialist. This is our coroner, Dr. Forsythe. Are you the owner of the house?"

Uncle Stuart nodded anxiously. "Yes … yes, I'm Stuart Randall. I'm the one who called."

"I understand you've uncovered what appear to be human remains in your backyard. Is that correct?"

"That's correct, Officer," Uncle Stuart croaked as he tried to clear his throat. "Come through here and I'll show you where it is." Officer Pratt and the other men followed Uncle Stuart through the house to the backyard. I nipped through the living room and out the French doors just in time to see my uncle point to the spot where the skull lay embedded in the earth.

Dr. Forsythe and Officer Pratt knelt and examined the skull without touching it. Then Dr. Forsythe took out two small tools. The first was a tiny paint brush, kind of like the one I had used earlier that morning when I painted a picture of my aunt's cat, Duff. The second was a sharp metal tool, like the pointy hook a dentist uses for cleaning teeth. He began gently brushing away the dirt with the paint brush. Just when I thought the waiting couldn't get any worse, he switched to the dental pick and started to remove tiny grains of dirt from the crevices. Finally, he nodded at Officer Pratt and stood.

"It's just what we thought it would be," Dr. Forsythe said, speaking casually while Aunt Margaret and Uncle Stuart hung back like crime victims. "What you have here is *not* a recently deceased individual."

"Oh, right, so now we're supposed to be relieved?" Uncle Stuart said. "Good news, honey. It isn't anyone we know!"

Dr. Forsythe and Officer Pratt smiled. "I take it you haven't lived in Crescent Beach long," Dr. Forsythe said. "You see, this entire peninsula was once a prehistoric Coast Salish village. By the looks of this skull, I'd say you have the remains of someone who lived and died on this land more than fifteen hundred years ago."

"Or even as long as five thousand years ago," Officer

Pratt added. "Unfortunately, accidental disturbances to ancient burials like this one have happened often over the past century in Crescent Beach."

Aunt Margaret's face was still ashen, and now Uncle Stuart's right eye was twitching. While they looked miserable, I felt as if I'd just won a lottery. Finding a dead guy in the backyard — well, that just had to mean something cool was about to happen. About time, too. I was starting to feel like Little Orphan Annie stuck in the middle of nowhere.

"You know, everyone has a few skeletons in their closet, but we're the only ones that have them in the backyard, too!" I quipped.

Officer Pratt chuckled, but Aunt Margaret wasn't amused. "Peggy, that's not an appropriate remark to make at a time like this."

Actually, I thought it was totally appropriate. Lots of people use humour to release tension at stressful moments.

"Oh, I just had a dreadful thought, Officer," Aunt Margaret said. "Do you think there are more dead ... ah, bones or skeletons around here?"

"Yes, ma'am, it's possible there are more prehistoric human or cultural remains in this area. But I hope you're not planning on digging them up."

"Certainly not, Officer Pratt." My aunt looked shocked. "But tell me, just what are we supposed to do now?" Her initial alarm had now turned to irritation.

"Don't worry, Mrs. Randall," Officer Pratt said. "Now that Dr. Forsythe and I have determined that this matter isn't a concern for contemporary forensics, we'll contact the Archaeology Branch in Victoria. They'll be glad to hear we have your assurance there will be no further disturbance to the remains until they can send someone to deal with all this. I'm sure the Archaeology Branch will also want to contact the nearest First Nations band."

"Did you say First Nations band? Why do the Indians need to get involved?" Whenever Aunt Margaret's voice got edgy like that, I made sure to stay out of her way.

"It's out of respect, ma'am," Officer Pratt said. "Any accidental discovery of human remains of aboriginal ancestry needs to be reported to the local First Nations people."

Uncle Stuart's face had turned red, and as he spoke his voice was a little jittery. "Sounds like we're getting into a lot of red tape. What happens next?"

"Well, then an archaeologist will come and determine what to do next," Officer Pratt said. "I guess in the future you might want to think twice before digging up your backyard." He grinned, but Aunt Margaret and Uncle Stuart didn't find him funny.

"So what were you making, anyway?" Dr. Forsythe asked.

"A pond," I blurted. Then I glanced at my aunt and uncle, whose faces were drawn and pale. "Well, look on the bright side. At least we weren't putting in a swimming pool!"

CHAPTER 2

The next morning I woke to the sound of voices coming from outside. When I glanced out the window, I saw a police car out front, along with a battered red pickup truck. A new cluster of people hovered on the opposite side of the street. I ran into my aunt and uncle's room, which overlooked the backyard. Through the window I saw Officer Pratt talking to someone dressed in a khaki safari shirt and pants, and a fishing hat covered in collector's pins.

The night before, Uncle Stuart had gotten a call from someone saying an archaeologist would be coming to the house in the morning. I didn't know much about what archaeologists did, except that they dug up old things. Once, I watched a movie with my mom called *Raiders of the Lost Ark*. She said it was a classic. The main character, an archaeologist named Indiana Jones, was always in and out of life-threatening adventures as he travelled around the world in search of ancient stuff for museums. But the chubby gnome standing in the backyard hardly looked like a daring treasure hunter to me.

I ran back to my room, threw on my favourite ketchup-stained Vancouver Canucks shirt and some shorts off the floor, then dashed downstairs. Just as I got to the back door, Aunt Margaret came in. "Oh, there you are. I was wondering how long it would take you to get down here."

I grinned as I brushed past her.

"Wait a minute! You're not going out looking like that!"

Too late — I was already leaping down the back steps three at time.

"Ah, here she is, my niece, Peggy," Uncle Stuart announced as I arrived at his side. "She was the first to recognize it was a skull. Peggy, you remember Officer Pratt from yesterday?"

I smiled at the officer.

"And this is Dr. McKay," my uncle added. "She's an archaeologist."

The stout figure bent over our pond hole straightened to greet me. "Please, just call me Eddy, short for Edwina. All my friends do."

My eyebrows were arched so high my forehead must have looked like corrugated cardboard.

"Bet you were expecting Indiana Jones in a fedora cracking a long whip!"

The adults beside me chuckled.

"No, not really. I just wasn't expecting you'd be an old lady." I heard my aunt gasp from behind. Then Officer Pratt laughed again.

"Well, I can understand what you mean," Eddy said. "Most blue hairs I know prefer digging around in their gardens instead of old burials." Then she smiled, and her warm eyes were like deep pools filled with unspoken words. She rested her hand lightly on my shoulder. "You seem to be a keen observer, Peggy. When I come back tomorrow, maybe you could help me excavate these remains."

"Sure," I blurted. Then I felt a sting of guilt about having called her an old lady. "I'd like to help. I mean, really, just tell me what to do and I'll do it!"

My aunt's voice cut through my excitement like a knife. "Well, now, just wait a minute. I'm not sure that's the kind of thing a child should be doing. Peggy's only twelve years old, Dr. McKay."

Aunt Margaret was my mother's older sister. I used to think she was cool, but that was before I came to live with her. She didn't have children of her own, and I think she had unrealistic expectations about what kids were really like. She was always asking in a critical tone, "Is that what your mother lets you do?" Or said stuff like, "I can't believe your mom lets you get away with that!" She didn't like my hockey jerseys, she was always giving me "logical consequences," and what was it with her and tidy bedrooms? And just because digging around in the dirt wasn't her kind of thing, it didn't mean she should stop me from having fun. Besides, they were just old bones; it wasn't like a real person.

"Maybe we should call Peggy's mom and see what she thinks," Uncle Stuart said. He flashed me a secret wink before Aunt Margaret shot him a piercing glare.

We all followed Eddy and Officer Pratt out front where the neighbours were still gawking from across the road. Aunt Margaret mumbled something to Uncle Stuart, but I only caught the last word — *embarrassing.*

"Okay, folks, there's nothing to be worried about," Officer Pratt said. "The Randalls have accidentally uncovered a prehistoric burial in their backyard and we've just finished securing the area. You should all go on home now."

After the officer's announcement, most people drifted away. By the expressions on their faces, it wasn't the kind of exciting news they were hoping to hear. Then I noticed this old guy leaning on the police car.

"Hey, Pratt, got any idea what phase it's from?" The man's voice was as gruff and gnarly as an old tree.

"Can't tell much yet, Walter," the officer replied. "We won't know anything until Dr. McKay finishes excavating."

The man turned to Eddy and growled, "McKay."

Eddy nodded back but didn't smile. "Mr. Grimbal."

Officer Pratt turned to Aunt Margaret and Uncle Stuart. "I'm surprised your new neighbour didn't tell you that Crescent Beach was a prehistoric village and burial ground."

"It's because we haven't met yet," Aunt Margaret said, holding out her hand. "I'm Margaret Randall and this is my husband, Stuart, and our niece, Peggy. We intended to get out and meet our neighbours, just not like this."

"Sure, I know how it is. I'm Walter Grimbal. I live around the corner on Agar." When he smiled, he revealed yellowed teeth. "I run the Real Treasures and Gifts store over on Beecher Street." Then he glanced at me. "I'll bet all this seems pretty exciting to a young lady like you."

I'd seen Mr. Grimbal's store but had the impression it was actually a junk shop. I smiled weakly as he put his cigarette-stained fingers on my shoulder. He smelled stale, like my room when it was filled with dirty old socks. Then I noticed a small hand-carved totem pole hanging around his neck.

"Walter here considers himself Crescent Beach's local expert on prehistoric Native people," Officer Pratt said.

"That's right," Mr. Grimbal said. "If there's anything you want to know about the ancient folks, just ask me." He raised his bushy eyebrows and gave another rotten smile.

"Well, I've got to get busy and write my report," Officer Pratt said. "I'm afraid you'll have to put your plans for a pond on hold for now, Mr. and Mrs. Randall."

"I hope it's not going to be too long. It's not our fault that our property's on top of an old burial." Aunt Margaret's voice cut to the point sharp as an X-ACTO Knife.

"We'll do what we can, Mrs. Randall," Eddy said politely. "In the meantime I'd better run along, too. I have a lot to prepare for our excavation." She shook my aunt's and uncle's hands and nodded cautiously at Mr. Grimbal. "I'll see you soon, Peggy."

After they left, Mr. Grimbal turned to Aunt Margaret. "Ah, too bad you got those sons of guns from the Archaeology Branch involved. You'll have old snooty-pants there prodding around for days, then someone from the band will want to come by … You'll be lucky if things are back to normal by the end of the summer. No pond, no backyard, no privacy!"

"Well, it would be safe to say I do have regrets — mostly that I ever got the idea of putting in a pond in the first place," Aunt Margaret said. "If you'll excuse me, Mr. Grimbal, I'm feeling a bit weary right now. I'm going to have a rest. Nice meeting you and I hope to see you again."

"Oh, you'll see me again," Mr. Grimbal growled in his raspy voice.

Uncle Stuart followed my aunt into the house, and I wandered into the backyard. I was glad to get away from Mr. Grimbal's awkward stare. I knelt by the gaping pond hole with its dark earth and partially exposed skull. Officer Pratt had said it could be as much as five thousand years old — and right here in our yard!

Gently, I rubbed my fingers over the smooth, sun-warmed skull. It reminded me of the time when my class was studying water mammals at the aquarium. We were each given a box of seal and otter bones that smelled rancid and felt gritty and greasy. But this skull was different. It felt more like the weathered driftwood scattered along the beach and smelled earthy.

I was scanning the yard for more signs of prehistoric treasures hidden under the thin blanket of earth when a sudden blustering wind caused the branches and leaves to wave and rustle frantically. For some reason I suddenly felt self-conscious, as if someone were watching me. I glanced around the yard and up to the windows, but there was no one. Gingerly, I walked up the stairs and resisted the urge to look back over my shoulder.

That night my mom called. Before I could talk to her, Aunt Margaret said she wanted some private time on the phone and then closed the door to her bedroom. I waited out in the hall, trying not to listen, but now and then my aunt's voice would go all shrill.

"Really, Liz, it's bad enough having this creepy thing in our backyard. I really don't think Peggy should ..." Then there was silence. I was dying to know what Mom was saying. I went into my room and quietly pushed the talk button on my telephone.

"And if anyone's the type to enjoy getting into a

dirt hole to excavate ancient bones, it would be Peggy," came Mom's voice from the other end. "She loves that kind of stuff. I know it's not your kind of thing, Margie, but it would really be good for Peggy. It's been tough for her this last while, and this is the kind of distraction she really needs."

I felt a flood of affection for my mom at that moment.

Aunt Margaret sighed. "Okay, Liz, I'll try it your way. I'll get Peggy now. I'm sure she'll want to hear what you have to say."

"Ah, I have the feeling she already has. Hello, Peggy, sweetheart, is that you on the other line?"

Moms — they know everything!

After I talked with my mother for a while, it was impossible to go to sleep. I was excited about helping Eddy with the excavation. The only thing I wasn't happy about was that Mom wouldn't be around to share the experience.

Moving to Crescent Beach with my aunt and uncle at the beginning of summer was part of my mom's plan to get me back to nature. She'd just finished reading *Unplugging Our Children from the Electronic Magicians* when Aunt Margaret and Uncle Stuart announced they'd bought a house near the beach.

"All the jobs are out east, Peggy," Mom had told me. "Given our circumstances, I think the best thing for you would be to stay here and live with Margie and Stu for a while. It will be the perfect opportunity for you to learn to appreciate the outdoors."

The part about learning to appreciate the outdoors was fine, because I really enjoyed nature. In the city, being "outdoors" meant busy streets, tall buildings, apartment blocks, and stores. In Crescent Beach it meant seeing the whole sky, smelling the salt and the seaweed from the ocean, hearing birds, the breaking of waves, and faraway voices. I loved everything about living in Crescent Beach — except it wasn't with Mom.

After about two weeks with Aunt Margaret, I pleaded with Mom to let me stay with Aunt Stella and Uncle Ron in Vancouver. They had four kids, and Nicky, their oldest, was my favourite cousin. But Mom figured it would be too much to ask them to take on another kid. So then I tried to get her to let me go to Golden to stay with Aunt Norma, who didn't have a husband or kids.

"Norma is far too busy with her work at the newspaper," Mom said. "She'd never be around to watch you."

Exactly! That was what would have made it so perfect.

At least the new house had given Aunt Margaret something to focus on besides me. She spent most of her time painting walls or picking out flooring or window covers. If it wasn't for that, I'd be her project. And since I started living with her, I'd discovered we hardly ever agreed on anything. Aunt Margaret thought I should be reading the classics, while I preferred mystery novels. She kept buying me icky pink and mauve outfits made of spandex to replace my comfy old hockey jerseys and skateboard T-shirts. And then she started talking about signing me up for pottery classes or guitar lessons so I could make new friends.

"Why can't she just let me decide what to wear or what to read or who to be friends with?" I complained to my mom on the phone one day.

"I guess she's forgotten what it's like being young. Give her time, pet. She'll come round."

Aunt Margaret's latest kick was making me do my own laundry. She said I needed to learn to look after myself. That was fine with me, because it meant she stopped coming into my room five times a day — even when there was a mountain of dirty clothes on the floor. I think she figured I'd give in when I had nothing clean to wear. But she didn't really know me that well. Every time I left the house wearing a wrinkled T-shirt and socks that didn't match, I could see her almost pinch her lips shut. I guess you could say I was giving her a crash course on parenting.

A few weeks after coming to live with my aunt and uncle, I got interested in collecting seashells. It started one day when I was sitting by myself at the beach. Mrs. Hobbs and her old basset hound, Chester, came along, their heads pointed toward the sand. They seemed to take no notice of the nippy southwest breeze coming in from the Pacific. I watched as the silver-haired lady stopped and bent down to examine something more closely. After brushing at some tiny object in her hand, she walked up to me as though we had known each other for ages and said, "Have you ever seen a more perfect specimen of an *Ophiodermella cancellata*?"

I had to agree that the white spiral-shaped shell with its delicate design was pretty, even though there was no way I could repeat its strange name.

"Well, here you are, young lady." Mrs. Hobbs placed the shell in my hand. "This can be the beginning of your collection. And the nice thing about shell collecting is

it's something you can do by yourself or with a friend."
Then she smiled and continued down the beach with
Chester waddling along.

After that I did start my own shell collection. And
whenever Mrs. Hobbs and I found ourselves at the
beach at the same time, we combed the sand together,
looking for more unique shells. Crescent Beach was
covered with limpets, and so far I had managed to find
four different species. I also had five types of snails,
two different butter clams, a Pacific gaper, and cockles
galore. But my favourite so far was the Adanson's lepton
with its pearly pink centre and purplish-red fringe. I was
planning to make a necklace with the shells for Mom
when I collected enough.

As soon as Aunt Margaret noticed I was interested
in shells, she bought me a book called *Shells of the Pacific
Ocean*. It had lots of beautiful pictures. At first I was
excited about the book. But then I realized it was her
way of taking control again — making shell collecting
into a "learning opportunity."

"You should label the shells in your collection with
their common and scientific names," she suggested one
day. "Then for fun you could look up their Greek and
Latin origins."

Right! That sounded like about as much fun as
watching twenty-year-old reruns of *Mr. Rogers*. Snore!

Whenever my aunt interfered, I tried to remember
she meant well. But I'd found the best thing was to stay
out of her way as much as possible. So when I wasn't
down at the beach collecting shells, I wandered past the
little shops and up and down the quiet streets. West Beach
had lots of fancy houses, like the ones along O'Hare

Lane. They had names hanging on signs out front like Swallow Hallow or Komokwa. I liked the name on the old Tudor house the best — Happy Haven. Sometimes there were garden parties with ladies in long dresses and men in suits drinking from tall, elegant glasses. No one seemed to notice when I stopped to watch.

The houses in East Beach, where I lived, were smaller. Most were cottages, built long ago, when people only came to Crescent Beach for their holidays. My aunt and uncle's house was nearly seventy years old and used to be a one-bedroom getaway. A previous owner added a second floor with three bedrooms.

One morning Aunt Margaret got the idea I should come with her to the decorating store and choose the paint colour for my bedroom. But I wasn't planning on living there for long and I certainly didn't want anything to do with picking out paint colours. I snuck out when she was in the shower and made my way to the end of McBride and out to the beach at Blackie's Spit. I liked early mornings on the beach the best. Hardly anyone was ever there.

A startled blue heron lurched awkwardly into the sky just as I jumped over a log and plunked myself onto the sun-warmed sand. I watched two seagulls fight over a cracked open clamshell, while two more circled silently overhead. I wondered how long it would take for the emptied clam to become tiny bits of crushed shell scattered all over the beach. On the other hand, it might go home in some kid's sand pail as part of a shell collection like mine, or become decorated with paint and glitter and sit on a windowsill.

On that morning Mrs. Hobbs and Chester were out

for a walk at the end of the spit. When she noticed me, she waved and marched in my direction. The wind whipped at strands of silver hair that had escaped from under her Tilley hat. And as the old dog waddled behind her, his tummy nearly dragged along the sand. Mrs. Hobbs lived on Sullivan Street, just down from Skipper's Fish and Chips. She once told me Chester liked to spend his free time sniffing out leftovers by the dumpster.

"Hello, Peggy. You wouldn't believe the treasure I've been gathering this morning!" Mrs. Hobbs said, nearly out of breath. She opened her palm and presented several long, thin tubular shells that were almost translucent, except for their pattern of tiny flecks. "These are tusk shells. With the tide out I managed to find these few in the mud and silt off the end of the spit. The ancient Coast Salish traditionally used them for decoration and trading."

"Trading?" I knew a shrewd bargainer never appeared too eager, so I tried not to look excited. "I'll trade you something for them."

"Hmm. What have you got that I might want?" Mrs. Hobbs's eyes were smiling.

"How about some of my best Adanson's leptons?" The tusk shells would be perfect for the necklace I wanted to make for Mom.

"That sounds pretty enticing. However, I was thinking more along the lines of, say, lawn cutting … next Saturday?"

"Sure. It's a deal! Thanks." I snatched the five delicate shells from her hand.

The day I got those tusk shells from Mrs. Hobbs was the first time I'd ever heard about the Coast Salish people. After Uncle Stuart and I discovered the skull in the yard, I realized those shells were the first sign of a strange adventure.

Now, since I couldn't sleep, I crawled out of bed and pulled down my shell collection from the shelf. I rolled the long tubular tusk shells in my fingers and thought about the ancient people and what Eddy had said about the burial. For the first time I was glad I had moved to Crescent Beach with Aunt Margaret and Uncle Stuart. Still, it would take some time getting used to the idea of living over an ancient Native burial ground.

Finally, I got back into bed and closed my eyes. I tried to imagine a time when the tiny peninsula was covered in trees and the only people were the dark-skinned Natives who lived by the sea.

CHAPTER 3

The next morning Eddy and I stood at the edge of the hole, looking down on the burial. She had already cleared away some of the dirt, and I could see a form beginning to emerge. It seemed more like a small child lying on its side, curled up in sleep. I felt a little weird staring at those fragile bones, bare of all life.

"Okay, Peggy, when excavating a site, what's more important at the time — the artifacts you find or the place you find them?"

In some ways Eddy reminded me of Mrs. Hobbs, though not in the way she dressed. Eddy wore a goofy hat covered in souvenir pins from all over the world and a khaki shirt with little pockets holding lots of little things, like a plumb bob, a measuring tape, and calipers. Her hands were thick and tough — the kind used to hard work and getting dirty. But she was easy to talk to like Mrs. Hobbs and made me feel as if what I thought mattered.

I searched for the words Eddy had used the day before. "It's the artifacts in … ah … situ — that's it! The artifacts in situ can tell you the most. That's why an archaeologist never takes the stuff out until every bit of information around the artifact has been recorded."

Eddy smiled. "What kind of information are we looking for?"

"Okay, I know this. How deep the things are from

the surface … ah, what other stuff is associated nearby … um, and what the layers of soil are like. That's the matrix, right?"

"All right! You've been listening! Now that you've passed the test you're ready to be my assistant." Eddy's round, wrinkled face smiled approvingly. Gently, she stepped over the string barrier she'd made and knelt by the bones. "Hand me the trowel and dustpan. I'm going to start by levelling this layer that you and your uncle started. Before we can remove the skull and bones, we have to see what else this burial can tell us."

I handed her the tool box. Many of the objects inside were things most people had in their garden shed — a dustpan, a bucket, a hand broom, and a diamond-shaped mason's trowel. There were also some plastic sandwich bags, a small paint brush, and a dental pick like the one Dr. Forsythe used.

Carefully, Eddy scraped the dirt into the dustpan "We're not planting flowers and shrubs, so it's important to consider that just millimetres below, or in the next scoop of matrix, we might find some important bit of information. We don't want anything to be damaged or missed." Eddy's pudgy body was perched over the burial as if she were a medic giving first aid. Occasionally, she stopped and wiped her forehead with the red bandana hanging loosely around her neck.

Soon the bucket was filled with black sandy soil dotted with bits of broken shell. "Okay, let's screen this stuff." She pointed to a rectangular frame covered in fine wire mesh dangling from three poles tied at the top like a teepee. "Once we've screened away the loose dirt, we'll look carefully for any small things I might have missed."

I struggled to carry the bucket over to the screening station. Every time I hoisted the pail up to dump its contents, the screen swung away. After three tries, I finally managed to empty the pail.

"We need to look for anything that appears to be plant life, small animal bones, or shell fragments that I can use to determine food sources available at the time of this burial," Eddy said. "There might even be some small artifacts, like flaked stone from tool-making."

I pushed around the cold, damp soil, which felt like coarse sandpaper to my hands.

"That-a-girl!" Eddy said. "Now push it around evenly and search for anything that might be important."

I studied the surface without recognizing anything special.

"Okay, nothing there," Eddy instructed. "Now start to shake it back and forth."

I rocked the screen as if it were a baby in a cradle.

"You'll have to do better than that," she told me. "Give it a good shake."

The tiniest grains of soil fell through, covering the plastic sheet with an ever-rising mound of dirt. I could imagine what Aunt Margaret was going to think when she saw all this dirt flattening her grass. Soon there was nothing left in the screen except some tiny pebbles and bits of broken shell that were too large to slip through the wire.

"It's nothing too exciting, but we'll bag these shell fragments as a food sample." Eddy brought out a clipboard, a paper form, and a plastic Ziploc bag. At the top of the paper were the words "Artifact Record Form." Below was the word *Site*, and next to it Eddy wrote "DhRr 1 — Peggy's Pond."

"These letters are a code that will tell any other scientist exactly which site this sample was taken from." Eddy winked. "Kind of like when *X* marks the spot on a pirate's treasure map."

"But why did you write Peggy's Pond?"

"It's customary to name a site. Sometimes we name it after the local Native group, or the landowner — or in this case the site discoverer."

My cheeks turned warm with colour, then I watched as Eddy wrote: "Shell samples are a possible food source, found in level 1, ten centimetres below datum." After that she filled the bag.

"Seems kind of gross that broken shell bits could be evidence of what ancient people ate, especially with a dead person in the mix," I said. "That's about as appetizing as finding the remains of a dead pet in the garden along with the zucchini and carrots."

Eddy chuckled. "I can see what you mean. But all these broken shells are here because the ancient ones heaped up the used clamshells or fish bones when they were finished with them — kind of like an ancient garbage dump, except it was all organic. Archaeologists call this a shell midden. We're not absolutely certain why, but it's quite common in this area to find burials in the midden."

"I bet it has something to do with covering the scent of the body so wild animals don't go digging it up. Nothing could stink as much as rotting fish guts and stuff, right?"

"That could be it," Eddy said, smiling. "All right, now that you've seen how we record information and store it in bags, you can do the next one."

She picked up the bucket and returned to the excavation pit. I knelt beside her on the grass, staring at the black midden like a pup ready to pounce on a ball.

The morning passed quickly, and I lost track of the number of buckets I screened. We didn't find a single artifact, and all there was to show for our hard work was a neat mound of loose sand, shell, and dirt under the screen.

"My legs are getting stiff," Eddy finally said. "How would you like to dig for a while?"

My heart leaped the way it had when Uncle Stuart said I could back the car down the driveway. Careful not to crush any fragile bones, I stepped inside the small pit. Moving around was a bit like trying to navigate inside a cardboard box.

"Remember," Eddy warned, "these bones and artifacts have been buried here for thousands of years, so go slowly and be gentle."

Okay, now that actually made me nervous.

I knelt and brushed away a thin layer of dirt dried by the sun. The bones were yellowy-brown, and I could see that some of them were badly cracked and crumbly.

"You're doing fine. And remember that an archaeologist needs to be patient." Eddy bent down and pointed to a spot near the top of the skull. "You see this here? I'm pretty sure it's some kind of a stone tool. It might even be a woodworking tool."

I could almost feel the pulse in my fingertips and had to resist the temptation to rip the stone out. My hand trembled as I scrapped around the artifact, then scooped and dumped the black earth into the bucket.

"Aha! You see, you see!" Eddy was crouched over the hole with her nose practically in the dirt. "It is a burin! Good job, Peggy!"

The object looked like any run-of-the-mill rock to me, except for the fluted edges that came to a point. "What's it for?" I asked.

"It's a tool we think was used for carving or engraving. You know what this means, don't you?"

I stared blankly.

"This is the first bit of cultural material that tells me this individual was quite likely a craftsman or a woodworker."

I was a bit confused. "That seems like a waste. It'd be like us burying a perfectly good skill saw with some guy just because he was a carpenter."

"You've got to remember, Peggy, that early people had a belief in an afterlife — much like people today. But in their case they wanted to make sure their friend or loved one had everything he or she needed for the next world, like tools, food, even jewellery. We call these grave goods."

"It sure would be nice if Peggy was as interested in keeping the floor of her bedroom as clean as this hole."

I quickly turned to see Aunt Margaret standing behind us. I had no idea how long she'd been there listening.

"Peggy, maybe Dr. McKay will let you borrow her broom and dustpan later. You never know what neat artifacts you'll find under all that dirty laundry." Even though she was smiling, I could detect a prickle of annoyance in her voice. "And before you come into the kitchen, make sure you scrub your hands with soap and water."

"I can assure you, Mrs. Randall, this is the cleanest dirt you'll ever find. And if Peggy keeps up the way she's been going, we may have ourselves a future archaeologist." Eddy gave me a thumbs-up.

"To be honest, I think she'd do better pursuing something else," Aunt Margaret said. "I don't imagine there's a big demand for archaeologists. By the way, I hope having her help you isn't slowing things down. Because I don't mind telling you that I can barely sleep at night knowing this … this … thing is out here."

Her nose wrinkled and her top lip curled as she wagged her finger at the bones in the ground. I wondered if Eddy had noticed how red my face had turned.

Eddy smiled at my aunt. "Well, that's just because you don't know him. Why don't I tell you a bit about our friend here?" Aunt Margaret's pinched face didn't relax, and Eddy must have sensed she had a lot of convincing to do. She bent over and gently picked up some of the bone fragments

"You see, an archaeologist reads bones like someone else might read the pages of a book. They tell us quite general things about the individual, like gender and height. But often there are other details etched into the bones like a primitive code that can tell us more intimate things — perhaps about a person's childhood, whether he had enough to eat, or what caused his death. It's a bit like being a detective who finds it's the tiniest details that can tell the most."

Some of the bones Eddy held were the size of a Tootsie Roll. But one was a sickly boomerang shape. "You see here? These phalanges or finger bones show a terrible case of arthritis. It must have made doing handiwork difficult. And the vertebrae in this spine are fused into a single carious bone, so it must have been pretty tough walking with a crooked old back like this." Eddy smiled at me and placed the curved spine in my hand. It was so fragile that dry fragments fell off and settled in the crease of my hand like crumbs of toast.

"We know that everyone was needed to contribute to the survival of the whole village, and for this poor soul, carving or basketry would have been difficult. But this burin here tells us that somehow he did it. The arthritis also strongly suggests this was an individual who lived a long life. Maybe he was an elder, a keeper of clan stories, perhaps a grandparent like me. And while he struggled to do his share of the work, all along he was probably in pain."

As the gnarled backbone rested in my hand, images flashed through my mind of an elderly man struggling along the sandy shores or down rooted forest trails.

"I know there are many differences between us and these ancient people," Eddy continued, "but I'm pretty sure we have a lot in common, too. They must have laughed at silly things, cried when someone they loved died, squabbled occasionally. But even during the tough times, every member of the village had an important job to perform, whether it was bringing in the fish, making baskets, or preserving food for the winter. So there wasn't much time for feeling sorry for yourself." Eddy took the fragile bones and put them back in the pit ever so gently as though trying not to cause them any further suffering. "And like everyone else, this poor dear had his place in the clan and his job to do."

"Hmm, that's very interesting, Dr. McKay," Aunt Margaret said without a hint of sympathy. "But it doesn't change the way I feel. I'll sleep better at night when it's out of my yard."

Blink! Her words had the same effect as a sudden power failure.

That evening I tried to call Mom on the phone to tell her about the excavation. I was desperate to talk to someone who cared about what I was learning. But her voice sounded tired, and she asked me to call back the next day. It wasn't like her to hang up without some kind of encouraging word.

After that I hid in my room. I wasn't in the mood to listen to Aunt Margaret complain about the mess in the yard, so I decided to organize my shell collection. At first I arranged them on my bed from largest to smallest, then reordered them into shell families. When that didn't seem right, I placed them in groups according to shapes. The tusk shells were the only long, thin shells in my collection. As I held them in my hand, I was reminded of the burial in the backyard. Eddy had talked about those old fragmented bones as if the man they had belonged to was someone deserving of respect. Then I recalled the stone tool. Eddy had called it a burin and had said it was used for carving. To her it was another clue, something to help her understand a prehistoric old man whose hands didn't work the way they used to.

I sat on the edge of the bed and closed my eyes. There, in the darkness of my mind, I began to see him. He had long grey hair that cascaded past his shoulders and down his bent old spine.

Far beyond the village the sun rests for a few moments on the mountaintops just before it slips behind them and into the sea. The people are getting ready for sleep inside the dark clan house. Many small pit fires burn low, and embers give off warmth and light. Some of the elders are already asleep on their cedar-bough beds. A few of the women rock and feed babies, while their men talk in hushed voices, clouds of smoke rising from their pipes.

The old man lies as comfortably as possible, propped slightly upon the bearskin rug at one end of the clan house. The children around him sit motionless, attention fixed the way the white-headed eagle watches for dinner.

"So Dark Sky wandered far and wide each night, searching for his courage." Shuksi'em speaks slowly, his deep voice rising and falling ever so slightly like the gentlest waves on a beach. "And every morning he returned to his village disappointed that he had failed to find it. We know he still searches to this day because every morning we wake to find the grass drenched in his tears."

The children gaze at Shuksi'em's wise old face ... knowing ... waiting ... for the story's life lesson. They have heard it many times already in their young lives, but each time is like the first, and they wait to gobble every word like baby birds swallowing worms from their mother's beak.

"It took great courage for the boy to wander alone in the woods each night, yet he thought he had failed in his mission. Someday you, too, will wander alone, struggling in the darkness, searching for the strength to face life's challenges. And when you do, remember to have faith in yourself. The courage you need is within you, waiting to guide you into the light."

Shuksi'em smiles, his eyes dancing with firelight. Slowly, he turns away to flatten his bed and lays his head down for sleep. One by one the children quietly creep off to their own beds somewhere close to a mother or father.

Feeling joy bubble up inside him, Shuksi'em smiles again. He enjoys his time with the children. They are filled with the promises of new life and none of the sorrows. Suddenly, a large, warm body pushes against his bent spine. It is a familiar shape that wraps around him like a shell to its clam.

"It seems like your stories grow longer every time you tell them, old man," Talusip says to her husband. "You should not forget that some of us need our sleep more than you."

"I, too, would like more sleep, but the damp mist of the night sneaks into my back and hands leaving me stiff with pain" Then Shuksi'em feels his wife's strong fingers gently pound and rub his crooked old spine until he finally drifts into a dream.

In the dream Shuksi'em returns from sea after many days. He is tired and ashamed that he has no catch of fish for his hungry clan. As he rounds the small finger of land only a short distance from his home, he suddenly thinks he has come to the wrong place — for the land is bare. He searches for a familiar sign, but even the clan house is gone. His heart thumps harder, faster. He is so weak now that he can hardly paddle his canoe. With no fish in the ocean to eat and no forest to provide food and shelter, how will his people survive? As Shuksi'em pulls his boat onto the shore, he feels himself dissolve into the sand.

When Shuksi'em awakes, the frightening images are still in his mind. But around him are the gentle sounds of the sleeping clan. And Talusip's body heat still seeps into his own. He is relieved that all is as it should be. As his fear slips away, his heart begins to settle and the rhythms of the night lull him back to sleep.

CHAPTER 4

It was almost nine o'clock when I crawled out of bed the next morning, but I felt as if I hadn't slept for more than a couple of hours. Slowly, I made my way downstairs, rubbing sleep from my eyes. I stopped midway when I heard a strange voice coming from the kitchen.

"It's too bad I didn't know about your plans for the backyard. I would have told you what could happen when you start digging in this town."

"It's been a terrible shock to my system, not to mention a real hassle," Aunt Margaret said. "I've spent hours planning the landscaping, and I can tell you this isn't what I envisioned for my garden."

"Well, next time you think about digging in your yard, just let old Bob give you some ideas about what to do with all that junk. Old bones make great wind chimes, and some of those artifacts are good as garden ornaments. I'll bet that skull you found would've made a humdinger of a conversation piece."

"Oh, please, don't remind me. I have a time trying to get to sleep knowing it's right outside my bedroom window." I could picture my aunt's face getting all dramatic.

"I can understand how you're feeling," the man said. "All the more reason you should get something for your trouble. After all, this is *your* place, not some old guy's who lived a couple of thousand years ago. It's *yours*, including everything on it."

Before I walked into the kitchen, I knew I'd dislike the man sitting at the table with my aunt. As I came through the doorway, Aunt Margaret smiled and her guest looked up from his coffee. He was a pear-shaped fellow wearing a T-shirt that read: RENO — WHERE MEN PLAY CARDS AND WOMEN SERVE DRINKS!

"Good morning, Peggy," Aunt Margaret said. "This is our new neighbour, Bob. He was telling me that people have been finding artifacts and bones around Crescent Beach for decades. He has some interesting ideas about what we should do if we find any more."

The man held out a pudgy hand. "Hi there! I'm Bob Puddifoot."

Just then I remembered seeing him before, but not face to face. Usually, when I passed by his yard, he was bent over his flower garden, his wide rump looking like two pillows. I shook his hand and smiled weakly. Then I turned away and poured myself some cereal. I noticed our town paper was open on the counter, and a big star was pencilled beside an ad that said: "Wanted: Ancient Native artifacts. Will pay good price. Contact 604-555-5555."

"Peggy has been helping the archaeologist, Dr. McKay, with the excavation," Aunt Margaret said. "It's a mystery to me, but she's quite keen on that sort of thing."

Bob chuckled. "Dr. McKay, eh? Now there's an odd duck. Most women her age are knitting booties for the grandkids, not digging up old bones and crusading around town playing advocate for people who've been dead for thousands of years."

"Excuse me, Aunt Margaret, but didn't Dr. McKay

say she'd be here a little after nine o'clock?" I asked, pretending to have forgotten.

Mr. Puddifoot grimaced. "Gads, is that woman coming here now? That means it's time I run along. Thanks for the coffee, Mrs. Randall. Nice to have met you, little girl." He snatched up his cap and hustled to the front door. Just before he walked out I heard him mumble to my aunt, "My gosh, there's no way I want to hear another one of Dr. McKay's lectures on respecting the dignity and rights of dead old Indians. Now don't forget what I told you about Walter. After all, this is your property."

"Why was he here?" I asked sharply after Mr. Puddifoot was gone.

"Peggy, that's a rather impertinent tone you're using. Mr. Puddifoot was just being friendly. He was concerned that we were getting pushed around and was explaining that anything we find on our own property belongs to us and we can do what we please with it — even sell it if we wanted."

"Except that those things don't belong to you."

"Just who do they belong to then? It's just a bunch of old bones and rocks."

Maybe my aunt had a point. I sat by the front window, waiting for Eddy to arrive, trying to reason it through. When the old pickup truck finally appeared, I darted out the back door and down the stairs. I moved the four large stones that held the plastic tarp in place over the large hole, then carefully folded the plastic back until the entire burial was exposed.

"Now aren't you an eager beaver. I'd like to see all my assistants as enthusiastic as you." Eddy was wearing her usual khaki shirt, but she had on a different hat. It was a forest green baseball cap that said: DON'S BACKHOES — WE DIG PEOPLE LIKE YOU! I felt a giggle inside me and thought about Mr. Puddifoot calling her an odd duck. She certainly wasn't like any grandmother I knew, even though I didn't know many grandmothers.

"So today we're going to continue working around the remains," Eddy said. "I've got a feeling we're going to find more burial goods that will tell us about our friend here."

I brought over the excavating tools from under the back stairs and handed Eddy the trowel and dustpan.

"Why don't you start where you left off, Peggy? You were doing such a good job yesterday that I think you should finish this level."

I felt like diving into the centre of Peggy's Pond. Instead I carefully stepped across the taut string that formed the border. Soon I was gently scraping dark soil into the dustpan and emptying it into the bucket. With every stroke I eyed the ground like a hawk hunting for prey. I remembered Eddy saying that every scoop of dirt might reveal another artifact or bone. The bright morning sunshine was heating the earth, and I could feel the warm air rising into my face.

After about ten minutes, my eye caught the pointy tip of a small greyish object protruding from the earth. Its shape and colour made it stand out from the speckled matrix.

"I think I found something, Eddy," I nearly yelled.

Eddy put down her notebook where she had been completing some drawings and came over. "Okay now, take the brush and clear away the dirt carefully." I gently swept around the object. "Oh, that's a beauty, Peggy!

You've got yourself a bone awl. That's another tool they used for piercing holes in leather or soft wood. Now take this ruler and set it beside the awl. Then I can take a picture of it in situ."

Just then I heard the scuffing sound of shoes on pavement coming up the walk behind us.

"Good morning, ladies," a distinctive raspy voice greeted. "Find anything interesting?"

Eddy and I turned to see Mr. Grimbal smiling down at us. His eyes found the bone awl in the ground.

"Look, Walter, I'm rather busy right now," Eddy said. "What do you want?" All the excitement in her face drained away as the tone in her voice became curt. She tried to move her body to shield the place where we had been looking at the artifact.

"Oh, I thought I'd come and see what's up," Mr. Grimbal said. "Got yourself a nice little awl there, I see." He came closer. "Looks like something from the Locarno Beach Phase, wouldn't you say, Doctor?"

"I wouldn't presume to say anything until all the data's in," Eddy said. "Peggy and I have a lot of work to do now, so you'll have to excuse us."

"Certainly. You carry on doing your thing." Mr. Grimbal smiled, but I could tell he wasn't trying to be friendly. "I just wanted to drop off my card — in case the Randalls decide to get in touch with me." He reached out his cigarette-stained fingers toward me with a small white business card wedged between them. "Give this to your aunt and uncle for me, will you?"

I quickly glanced at the words written on the front: "Real Treasures and Gifts, Mr. Walter Grimbal, owner and proprietor, 11228 Beecher Street, Crescent Beach, B.C."

Underneath, in smaller print, it said: "Specialist in Native Artifacts." I stuffed the card into my pocket and turned my attention back to the awl.

"It's a nice piece you got there, kid," Mr. Grimbal said. "Probably worth a pretty penny."

Eddy didn't take her eyes off Mr. Grimbal. She stared at him hard as if trying to turn his gaze away from the artifact on the ground.

"Right then, be seeing you soon." He smirked and walked out of the yard.

It was as if Mr. Grimbal had come by just to wave his red cape at Eddy, as if she were a bull in the ring. Though it took her a few minutes to calm down, she was soon breathing evenly again and her face relaxed.

"That old pirate's always looking for a way to turn ancient artifacts into a scheme for making money, Peggy. You'll have to be careful about what you say around him." Eddy wiped her face with her bandana and smiled weakly. "Okay, let's get a picture of this fine tool and take some measurements. Then we can remove it and put it somewhere safe."

I wondered if what she really meant was to put it somewhere safe from Mr. Grimbal. "Eddy, do you think Mr. Grimbal would ever come and steal any of the artifacts from this burial?"

She wiped the dirt from her hands onto her pants and then set the aperture on the camera. "Have you ever heard about the grave robbers in Egypt who went into almost every ancient tomb and looted all the treasures and nearly destroyed everything else while they were at it? They did that because they had no idea that one day the tombs and all their contents would come to mean so much to the entire world. They could only see as far as the moment they were in. Well, that's Walter Grimbal — a grave robber who doesn't have any respect for the ancient people or the science of archaeological excavation.

"He's not a bit interested in helping to preserve the past for us all to learn from and enjoy. He'll sell prehistoric hand-carved stone tools and other artifacts to people who just want to use them for bookends or trinkets." Eddy's voice had become loud and her round cheeks had turned bright red. "So do I think Walter would come and steal artifacts? I think you know the answer." She shook her head as if she were trying to shake off a cloud of gnats. "Let's just forget about him and get back to this wonderful discovery."

After Eddy photographed and measured the bone tool from all possible angles, she put the artifact into a marked clear plastic bag and then into a small metal box. "Okay, now that the awl's tucked safely away, let's get back to work."

I followed Eddy back to the excavation pit.

"Before we get started," she said, "I'm going to test your observation skills. Take a close look at the skull, look down around the jaw. Do you see anything curious?"

I must have looked surprised by the question.

"Well?"

I got down on my hands and knees and examined the skull closely. It was yellowy and cracked in several places. The teeth were worn down almost to the roots, and they were all brown and pitted. Then I noticed that most of the skull's surface was uniformly smooth — all except a small knob where the upper and lower jaws met.

There it was all bumpy.

"This looks kind of weird," I said, tentatively pointing to the knob. "It's like it's been eaten away by battery acid or something."

"That's a great observation, Peggy, and a good description, too. That's his mastoid process. It seems like our friend here had a case of mastoiditis, which is a fancy way of saying a really bad ear infection. It's the kind of problem that could have caused him to lose his hearing in that ear."

I'd never really had an earache, but I winced at the thought of it. I looked back at the teeth next to the corroded mastoid process. They were so foul-looking that I was suddenly glad for all those times my mom had hounded me to brush my own teeth twice a day.

"Why are his teeth so bad?" I asked. "And don't say it's because he never flossed them before bed."

Eddy chuckled. "Well, that kind of tooth erosion was probably caused by a couple of things. One reason has to do with the way they processed their food — a lot of sand and dust got in when they used grinding stones to break it down. But there's also something else going on." She took her pencil and pointed at the molars. "Notice how worn down they are — and not in a usual way, either. These deep grooves on each side are a peculiar wear pattern. I believe it comes from using the teeth as a kind of tool. Because of his crooked spine, there's a good possibility that hunting and fishing were impossible for this individual. So he might have had to resort to women's work — basket making, for instance."

"What do his worn teeth have to do with basket making, Eddy?"

"Good question. The women used various plants and bark for weaving baskets. For instance, cattails are prolific around here and are great for weaving. But first the stems needed to be softened, and molars are perfect for such a job. But, of course, you can see the drawback — terrible wear and tear on the teeth."

Soon Eddy and I were back at work. For the rest of the morning I dug and screened while she drew, wrote, and recorded. It was past lunchtime when Eddy finally took out a brown paper bag from her knapsack and sat on the grass. "You'd better get yourself something to eat, too, Peggy."

I was glad for the break, because my stomach had been making noises for the past hour. I ran up the back stairs and into the kitchen. Aunt Margaret was upstairs talking to someone on the phone. I got myself a couple of slices of multi-grain bread and slapped on a heap of peanut butter. Then I cut up a couple of pickles and some onion slices and placed them on top. Peanut butter sandwiches always made me think of Mom. She always said everything went with peanut butter.

"Hmm, another one of your delicious creations!" Aunt Margaret said sarcastically as she came into the kitchen.

"Want some?" I offered.

"Ah, no, thank you. So you and Dr. McKay are taking a break, are you?"

I nodded and tried to talk, but there was too much peanut butter stuck between my tongue and the roof of my mouth. The best I could do was move my head and mumble.

"I was just talking to your mom," she said.

My eyeballs nearly popped out of my head as I shot Aunt Margaret a fierce look.

"I know you've been waiting to talk to her, but she's not in a good mood right now. She just got turned down for that job she was hoping to get, and she's feeling pretty discouraged. Why don't you give her a call tonight to cheer her up?"

That was the kind of thing that really bugged me about my aunt. Who was she to decide when or if I should talk to my mom?

After I finished my sandwich, I shuffled back out to the yard and sat by Eddy on the lawn. She was stretched out on the grass and had her eyes shut. I was glad we didn't have to talk. I had been trying to get in touch with my mom for two days, and I was really beginning to worry about her.

My mom liked to pretend she could handle any problem. I knew she just wanted to keep me from worrying. She always said, "Kids shouldn't have to worry about stuff. They should be carefree." But the fact was I did worry — mostly about her. Like did she have enough money? Was she eating properly? What kind of a place was she staying in? Was she lonely? I knew I had learned to live without my dad, but I didn't think I could handle being without her, too. If I didn't think about something else quick, though, my face was going to get all puckered and I'd start bawling. I didn't want Eddy to see me like that.

My eyes wandered over the old bones and the yellowed skull in the pit. Maybe the old guy had had a tough life, but he had nothing to worry about now. I stretched out on the grass beside Eddy and closed my eyes, too.

Shuksi'em feels frustrated with his thick, stiff fingers. He has been trying to carve an alder ceremonial bowl, but when the pain in his hands comes there is nothing he can do but wait for it to pass. Behind him all the women, except his wife, are making new dipping fish nets. Talusip is working on a water basket made from spruce root.

"Come, old man, and help me soften these root fibres. I need them to make the string for my basket." But Shuksi'em does not hear his wife as the wind blows into his one good ear. She throws a pebble at his back. He cannot turn his head to look at her, but a grunt tells her he is listening.

"Oh, you are an old snail," she says. Talusip takes up her half-finished basket and roots and crawls to her husband's side. "Here, if you cannot carve today, you might as well help me." She hands him a hand-sized stone and some roots. He begins to pound steadily. When the fibres are ready, he will rub them against his thigh until they entwine and become strong, supple pieces.

"Later I will get you to soften some cattails," the old woman says. "I will use them for decoration. You must grind them with your teeth, though."

"Woman, there is little left of my teeth," Shuksi'em mutters. "I think it best to save them for grinding my food."

Down on the shore, where the river meets the bay, Shuksi'em can see the black heads of the young men bobbing in excitement. They must have a big catch of the pink fish today. He envies their straight and strong bodies.

"Once I was tall and straight and people called me Tall Cedar when I walked by," Shuksi'em tells his wife, as if it were a fact she did not already know.

Her laugh is brittle with age. "Well, you must have

*angered the sneaky raven greatly for him to come and steal
your body away, leaving you with a back that winds like a
river and hands stiff as bear hide."*

The old man breathes deeply when a gust of wind brings
the smells of the forest to him. Even more than fishing, he
longs for the days when he walked with the other hunters
among the tall fir, hemlocks, and cedars. Sometimes they
would come upon a huge ancient tree of their ancestors.
At times like that the men would proudly join hands and
embrace the giant tree, thanking the Great Spirit for this
sign of his power and abundance. Then they would rest
in the forest until it was time to silently creep out to the
meadow of white-tailed deer.

CHAPTER 5

After Eddy left for the day, I decided to head to the beach. I knew Aunt Margaret would want to mess around with my head, checking out how I was feeling about my mom's bad news. But there was no way I'd talk to her about it, no chance I'd let her analyze me. Cutting through the path that led past the sailing club and out to Mud Bay, I found an old log worn smooth by years of rain, sun, and wind and rested my back against it. It was nearly suppertime, and the place was almost deserted.

Even though I had managed to push her to the back of my mind all afternoon, Mom was never really out of my thoughts. Now that I was alone, I let myself think about how much I missed her. It felt like years since we'd been together and she had pinned me in one of her bear hugs. My heart beat harder and my eyes started to water.

"Hello, young lady. I was wondering when I'd see you again."

I recognized Mrs. Hobbs's voice coming from behind me and quickly rubbed my eyes. Just then Chester waddled over to me and plopped his wet, sandy snout on my arm. I pulled it away and rubbed his gob on my shorts.

"Would you like to search for more of those tusk shells with me, or are you too tired from all that excavating?" Mrs. Hobbs asked.

I was surprised she knew about it. I hadn't seen her

for over a week.

"This is a small town, Peggy. News spreads faster than cow patties." As she looked at me, her eyes turned into warm pools of concern. "Perhaps this isn't a good time, dear?"

I didn't have a grandmother, but if I did, I'd want her to be just like Mrs. Hobbs. Suddenly, I felt the warm trickle of tears on my cheeks. It made me angry that I was crying, and I tried to fight it off.

"You just go ahead and let those tears flow, Peggy. Sometimes the best thing we can do for ourselves is to have a good cry. It helps when we're worried about some problem to let out all that emotion."

After a few minutes, my head was pounding and my eyes stung from all the salty tears. When Mrs. Hobbs handed me a tissue, I wiped my face dry, then sniffed. "Thanks, Mrs. Hobbs. I'd really like to collect shells with you. Could we do it after supper? I know my aunt's expecting me to come home to eat soon."

"I don't think the light will be so good after supper, but I have an even better idea. Why don't you come by and we'll get started on that shell necklace for your mother?"

I jumped up off the sand and almost tripped over Chester, who was gnawing on some driftwood beside me. "That would be great, Mrs. Hobbs! I'll bring over my collection."

She gently swept her warm, soft hand across my face and smiled. Her unexpected affection almost made me start crying again. "All right then, my dear. I'll see you after dinner."

When I got back to the house, I found a note on the kitchen table:

Peggy, Uncle Stuart and I are making a trip to the garden store. We're going to price koi fish for our pond — for whenever it finally gets done! I don't appreciate your leaving without letting me know where you're going. We'll talk about that when I get home. There's a grilled cheese sandwich and a bowl of soup waiting to be warmed up in the microwave. Uncle Stuart made it, so I can't promise you how it's going to taste. We'll be back by 8:00.

— Aunt M

Good, I had the place to myself for once. I put the microwave on, then dashed upstairs to my room to get my box of shells. When I tripped over the clothes scattered on the floor, I was reminded that one of these days I should wash them. After my supper was ready, I ate on the porch overlooking the backyard. My eyes were dry and sore from crying, but I felt a lot better. Mrs. Hobbs was right. I guess a good cry really did help. I polished off the last of my soup and sandwich and was getting up to leave when Duff rubbed against my leg.

"Sorry, boy, you're too late. I ate it all." I scratched the orange tabby under the chin, but he seemed annoyed with me and took off down the stairs. He glanced up at me, then sauntered over to the orange tarp protecting the burial. Just as he was about to walk across it, I yelled, "Get out of there, Duff!" My sudden outburst startled him. Then he narrowed his eyes, flicked his tail at me, and marched toward the gate as if I'd hurt his feelings.

Before leaving for Mrs. Hobbs's house, I tried calling my mom in Toronto. Because of the three-hour time difference I wanted to talk to her before she went to bed. After several rings, the motel operator came on the line and asked if I wished to leave a message. I said no and hung up. Maybe Mom was having one of her famous long, hot baths. I would try again later.

Soon I was walking up Mrs. Hobbs's garden path with my box of shells tucked under my arm. When I got to the front porch, the door was slightly ajar. The smell of baking seeped through and grabbed me by the nose. I knocked gently and pushed the door open. "Mrs. Hobbs, I'm here."

"Oh, hello, Peggy dear. Come in. I'm in the kitchen."

I wandered into the room where mixing bowls, measuring spoons, and bags of flour and sugar cluttered the counter.

"I thought we should have something nice for our work party, so I've baked us some double chocolate chip cookies," Mrs. Hobbs said.

"My favourite!" I said approvingly, sitting at the kitchen table. "I brought my shells like I said. But I don't think I have enough to make a necklace yet."

"Behind you, on the china hutch, is a box," she told me. "That's it. Take a look inside."

I pulled the metal fisherman's tackle box from the polished mahogany chest and opened it. Inside were hundreds of tiny shells of all kinds sorted into compartments. Immediately, I noticed the neat stack of tusk shells.

"I've been collecting shells for a long time, Peggy, and I've been waiting for someone like you to come along and make use of them."

A smile streaked across my face, and I knew this was how it felt to visit a grandma.

"Well, let's begin, shall we?" Mrs. Hobbs pulled over a large stack of books that was sitting on the table. Each book had several paper markers. She picked the top book off the pile and opened it about halfway. "Take a look at this one, Peggy."

The picture was black and white and seemed very old. I was fascinated by the unsmiling, young Native woman staring out from the page. She wore a long, wide band of tusk shells, mixed with smaller round shells over top of what appeared to be a poncho. The woman had a wide face with high cheekbones and a squared jaw. Though her skin looked smooth, she had deep creases around her eyes — like laugh lines. Crow's feet, Mom would have said. And her hair was parted in the middle and braided along each side of her face. But it was her dark, magnetic gaze that held my attention.

Mrs. Hobbs showed me other pictures and necklace patterns. Some were made of beads and feathers, others of shells, porcupine quills, and bones. But I had already decided I'd make a necklace like the one worn by the lady with the penetrating eyes. Her necklace must have had over a hundred tusk shells. Mine would have to be narrower.

"Mrs. Hobbs, I think I'd like to make a necklace like this one." I pointed at the picture. "Only I won't be able to make it as wide. And I'm thinking of using up my Adanson's leptons in between to fill it out more."

Mrs. Hobbs studied the picture thoughtfully. "Yes, you could do that, Peggy dear. But rather than put holes in your lovely leptons, we could use shells that have natural holes." She pulled out a couple of shells and placed them in her hand for me to see. "This here is a two-spot keyhole limpet, and the other is a littleneck clam with a hole drilled by a moon snail. The tusk shells already have holes at each end, so it would simply be a matter of threading them all."

I had my heart set on using my Adanson's leptons, but maybe for my first necklace it was better to go with the simpler plan. "I guess I could use these keyhole limpets, Mrs. Hobbs. I think the littlenecks are too big for what I have in mind."

"Okay, then. And we can use this fishing line to string them together. Of course, the ancient people wouldn't have had this. They'd have made their necklaces with leather cords, or twine from cedar trees or strands of woven human hair." Mrs. Hobbs pulled out a tray with tiny coloured beads. "You can add a few of these for colour, if you like, though traditionally they wouldn't have had anything like this." She helped me get my necklace started, then turned back to the books to look for a pattern of her own.

Before long my fingers seemed to have a mind of their own as I strung the shells and beads. And for the first time in a long while I felt safe and comfortable, like the nights Mom and I curled up together in bed and read. As I worked, I thought about the stunning face in the book and wondered what the woman was thinking as she had stared down the lens of the camera nearly a hundred years ago.

"Mrs. Hobbs, if you found an artifact on your property, what would you do with it?" I could see that she was thinking about the question before answering. "The reason I was asking," I went on, "is because this weird guy came over to our house. He owns the gift shop in town and buys and sells ancient artifacts. I even saw his ad in the paper this morning. Our neighbour, Mr. Puddifoot, and Aunt Margaret seem to think it's okay."

"The gift shop owner you're talking about is Walter Grimbal." I guess I shouldn't have been surprised that she knew who I was talking about. "Well, honey, Mr. Grimbal hasn't had an easy life, and I think it's left him hard and indifferent. But in my mind those artifacts he sells should never belong to just one person. They're part of our prehistory. If they can't stay in the ground with their original owners, then they belong in a museum where everyone can enjoy them."

"You sound like Eddy. She's the archaeologist who's been excavating the burial in the backyard."

"Oh, heavens, no need to explain who Eddy is. We go back a very long time — back to about your age, I imagine." Mr. Hobbs chuckled over the surprised look on my face.

"You were friends?"

"Our mothers were good friends. As a child, I liked her all right, and she probably thought I was all right, too. We just didn't have much in common. We both spent the summers here in Crescent Beach. I lived in Vancouver, and she came from New Westminster. Those were the days when Crescent Beach was a ghost town in the winter and only came to life at the start of summer vacation. I was more interested in playing imaginary games or dressing up in Mother's party gowns. Edwina, well, she was more like you." Just then Mrs. Hobbs bent down and patted Chester's flat head. He was asleep under the table at our feet. "What a lovely, smelly old thing you are, dear."

"So ... what about now?" I asked.

"We don't see each other often, but there's certainly a warmth from our shared past. And I realize now that we did have something in common — our love for Crescent Beach. Edwina loves this place because of its rich prehistory — and it's where she first learned about archaeology. And I love it for all the other reasons — the peaceful walks along the beach, the friendly, small-town feel of the place, and of course the birds! I've spent many hours out on Blackie's Spit waiting for a glimpse of a heron, a red-winged blackbird, or a dove-tailed finch."

Mrs. Hobbs walked over to the stove and took out another batch of cookies from the oven. "But when I was your age, what I really loved about being here was sailing out in the bay with my brother, Charlie. We had a little sailboat, and almost every day we'd pack a lunch and stay out on the water for hours. There were times when we infuriated our mother. She'd stand on the shore calling us in, but we'd pretend we couldn't see or hear her." Mrs. Hobbs giggled as if she still remembered what it felt like to be a kid. I giggled also when I imagined myself far from shore while Aunt Margaret waved hopelessly for my attention, too distant to give commands or lectures about being responsible.

Gazing out her window, Mrs. Hobbs smiled. "Oh, dear, we certainly did have the most wonderful summers a child could have. Days before it was time to pack up and return to the city, I'd spend every waking moment sailing, swimming, or walking the beach and collecting shells. In fact, I wouldn't be surprised if some of those shells in my collection are ones I got long ago."

After a while, Mrs. Hobbs and I fell into a comfortable silence as we worked and I let my thoughts drift away like a tiny boat on the water.

It is morning, and Shuksi'em steps out from the dark, smoky clan house. The warm morning sunlight sweeps over his bare chest like a blanket of soft eagle feathers. The stiff, dull throb in his arms and back begins to fade away under its gentle caress. Pain or not, he thinks this is the best part of each day — behind him the silence of the sleeping clan, before him the rhythmic lapping of the waves on the sand. Carefully, he steps down from the lodge entry with the help of his walking stick made from a sturdy cedar branch. He walks slowly and deliberately toward the water, thinking of the events this new day may bring.

Some of the women and children will gather more of the delicate pink berries that look like salmon eggs. They are a small joy on a summer's day and a sweet reminder in the cold of winter. Shuksi'em rubs his hungry belly at the thought of the delicious cakes the women will make from mashed berries and seaweed. These small delicacies are like candy as they slip from their moulds slick with fish oil.

At the shore Shuksi'em stands just close enough so that the waves wash over his feet. The cool water sends a shiver up his bent old spine. Later, when the tide pulls the waves away from the shore, the villagers will dig for clams, mussels, and seaweed. He hopes Talusip will prepare his favourite dish for their evening meal — limpets and mussels soaked in tasty fish oil.

With the help of his cedar stick to lean on, Shuksi'em bends his knees until he is close enough to fall gently to the sand. It takes great effort, but he manages to stretch his neck so he can gaze across the bay to the land and the giant mountains beyond. He knows the young men are nearly ready for the big hunt and may even leave tomorrow. Soon there will be fresh deer meat, and if the men are lucky, succulent elk or bear. This is the season when every meal is like a feast and his old bones get padded with extra flesh.

Shuksi'em does not hear the gentle swish of the sand as Talusip approaches, though he senses her before her hand rests upon his grey head. He grunts gently to acknowledge her presence.

"Ah, another good day for gathering." She yawns and stretches before she eases down beside her husband. "You did not sleep well again last night, Husband. Would you like some spruce tea to ease the stiffness?"

She is a good woman, Shuksi'em thinks as he shakes his head.

"Q'am says he will take the boy with him on the big hunt. I say it is too soon, but he will not listen. You should talk to him. He listens to you."

Shuksi'em's stiff backbone will not allow him to turn his head to face her, but she sees his smile from the side. "You said the same to me when I took Q'am out to the hunt for the first time." His voice falls silent as he thinks back to that day. "We both know the journey of life is often dangerous. You and I have travelled a long way on its path together. Whether we went slow with cautious steps or raced along fearlessly, we have always known it was not us who decides when the journey will end. Q'am is a good father to the boy, and I say we let him do what he thinks best for our grandson."

"Old man, do you ever have a simple answer? After all these seasons together, it would be nice if sometimes you would just agree. But that is not possible for you. No, no, no!" Talusip slaps teasingly at his bare arm but does not hurt him.

Shuksi'em smiles at his good wife. He knows why her heart is filled with fear. The clan has lost many of its young over the years. Some died on the hunts or out on the ocean when the waters turned angry. Then there were many seasons of terrible sickness, and the clan lost many children, including two of their own young ones.

Talusip rolls onto her side like a round sea lion and pushes herself up. Before she leaves she strokes Shuksi'em's long silver hair. "Don't forget, Husband. You promised your granddaughter you would help her design a necklace for the fall ceremony."

With his wife gone, Shuksi'em steals back to the last few peaceful moments of the morning. Behind him, at the forest's edge, the families are beginning to stir and will soon emerge from the clan lodge. He pushes his rough, rigid hands past the sun-warmed surface to the cool sand below. Over and over, he churns up the warm and the cold, the dry and the wet. Then he lets the sand sift through his thick, leathery fingers until all that remains are a few small spiral shells. They will not do. He will need something special for this youngest grandchild.

When it is time for the fall spirit dance, the guests will come to the village for the feast. The elders are to announce each daughter's passage to womanhood. Shuksi'em wants his granddaughter, Sleek Seal, to sparkle brighter than the dew in the morning's light. He will send her mother out to the flat, muddy shore around the bend to search for the precious tusk shells.

I'd had a great time with Mrs. Hobbs, and I'd made a good start on my shell necklace, too. When the light began to fade outside, I knew I'd soon have to go home.

Mrs. Hobbs beamed. "You've made wonderful progress, Peggy dear. And if you want, you can come tomorrow and work on it some more. I don't mind telling you that I'm glad to have your company."

I felt the same way.

As I walked home, I was all warm inside. But when I entered the house I was hit by a wave of tension. Aunt Margaret was talking on the phone, and her voice pierced the air. "Oh, here she is. Honestly, that child needs to learn to be more responsible and considerate. I want you to tell her that this kind of thing is definitely not okay with me! She just wanders off, God knows where, and never thinks about telling someone where she's gone. You need to talk to her." Then she angrily shoved the phone at me. "Peggy, it's your mother."

I was glad when Aunt Margaret stormed out of the room. "Hi, Mom."

"Hello, Peggy. Your aunt's very upset with you for leaving the house again without telling her where you were going. She's been worried."

"How was I supposed to do that? She wasn't here at suppertime. She was out shopping for pond fish."

"You could have written her a note, or stayed home until she got back. Or why didn't you call from wherever you were?"

"Yeah, I guess I could've done that. But then she'd have found a way to ruin my plans."

"Well, where did you go?"

"I was with Mrs. Hobbs. I'm making something,

but it's a surprise, so I can't tell you about it."

"Well, honey, I can't see why Margaret wouldn't let you visit Mrs. Hobbs. But next time you need to get her permission before you go out. She's only trying to do her best to look after you. And I shouldn't need to remind you that she's doing us a big favour."

"Mom, I feel like she's trying to squeeze the life out of me. She has so many rules and she always has to tell me what to do. We have nothing in common. She doesn't even care about the excavation Eddy and I've been working on. She keeps dropping reminders of what a hassle it's all been for her. When are you coming back, Mom?" There was a long, awkward silence.

"I can't say right now, sweetheart. Hey, why don't you tell me what you've been learning about archaeology and excavating?"

She had totally ignored my question. I would have pressed her, but her voice sounded funny, as if she'd been crying. "Yeah, it's pretty cool," I said, trying to sound cheerful. "But I wish you were here to see it." There was another long, silent moment, and sniffling noises came from inside the phone.

"There's nothing I'd like better, honey, but I'm afraid it's not possible right now. I didn't get that job at Cobblestone Communications. And I was really counting on it, since money's getting tight." More silence. "But don't worry, Peggy. I'll find a job soon. And the moment I do, I'm coming to get you, okay?"

It was bad enough that Mom was feeling down for not getting the job. I didn't want her to worry about me, too. "No problem, Mom. I'm fine and I'm happy to be here. Just take care of yourself." There was a really long silence this time, and I could actually hear her sobbing. "Mom, please don't cry. Everything's going to be all right."

"Good night, Peggy," Mom's voice squeaked, and then I heard a click as she cut the connection.

I had a hard time sleeping and spent most of the night thinking about my mom, crying, alone in some motel room, far from everyone she loved. I must have fallen asleep for a while, but woke up to a large, wet spot on the pillowcase. I turned the pillow over and dried my tears with the back of my hand. For the first time in years I felt angry at my dad for dying.

CHAPTER 6

"Good morning, Peggy. It's time to get out of bed."

My aunt's stern voice startled me awake.

"Things need to change around here, and I'd like to start with this bedroom. Before breakfast it must be cleaned and your dirty laundry has to be taken downstairs."

"Yeah, okay." I looked around my room and admitted to myself that it had gotten a little out of control.

"And another thing. You have far too much free time on your hands. You need some structure, so I called up the Crescent Beach Sailing Club. They just started a new class a few days ago, but the instructor said it's not too late if you start today."

"But that will interfere with the excavation," I argued.

"You're a twelve-year-old girl. You don't know what's best. Besides, what child wouldn't want to learn to sail?"

"Me!" As soon as I replied, I thought about what Mrs. Hobbs had said about sailing — about being so far away that her mother couldn't tell her what to do.

"Well, anyway, it's a chance for you to make some friends."

So that was it! "I have friends," I said, trying to sound normal. I hadn't forgotten what Mom had said last night.

"Yes, well, I think you're spending far too much

time with senior citizens. You need to meet someone your own age."

Silently, I apologized to my mom before I opened my mouth. "How would you know? I bet you can't even remember what it was like being a kid. Mrs. Hobbs and Eddy might be old, but they know a lot more about kids than you do."

My aunt's eyes nearly jumped out of their sockets. Then she turned and went out the door. I'd won! Or so I thought.

"Get ready to go," she said as she stomped downstairs. "They're expecting you in half an hour."

How could she decide something like that without even asking me? Who did she think she was? "Well, what if I don't go?" I yelled back.

"Then you can say goodbye to spending time excavating with Eddy or visiting Mrs. Hobbs."

A half-hour later I stormed out of the house and headed up Sullivan and then right on McBride. I hadn't bothered to brush my hair, and I knew my aunt had seen me leave wearing my ripped skater T-shirt, the one she said I could only wear around the house. I thought about skipping the sailing lessons and going to Mrs. Hobbs for the day, but Aunt Margaret was probably planning to check up on me.

I was so angry that I broke into a run and sped down the road. When I arrived at the sailing club, I was out of breath and gasping. Then I noticed a tall guy standing in the doorway of the clubhouse. His skin was so tanned and shiny that he reminded me of an oiled hot dog.

"Hey, there, you must be Patty. I'm the sailing instructor — Vic Torrino. But the kids just call me

Tornado. Get it? Torrino, Tornado!"

I tried to tell him that my name wasn't Patty, but he only started to babble some more.

"Good to see you're an early bird. That's a good sign. It's like that saying … something about the early worm."

"It's the early bird that catches the worm," I said, doing my best not to let my voice betray the venom I was still feeling.

"Yeah, that's what I meant." He flashed a smile so brilliant that he looked like one of those models in a poster for a toothpaste commercial. "Hey, here comes Melissa and Jennifer. Good morning, girls."

"Same, Tornado," chimed the two teens, who looked as if they had lurched out of a plastic doll commercial as they pranced up the sidewalk.

"This here's Patty," Tornado said. "She's joining the class today."

The girls glanced at me for a microsecond. "Cool," the tall one said as if I were a dead fly.

Were these the kind of kids Aunt Margaret had in mind when she'd said I needed to make friends my own age?

"You can learn a lot about sailing from these two," Tornado said. "It's their second time taking my class, which makes them a good example of determination, too. Like that saying, if at first you don't succeed, get back up on the horse."

I didn't know how, but I was going to get my aunt back for this.

The next couple of hours were about as much fun as I'd expected. We looked at a video on the importance of always wearing life jackets while boating. And then we spent an hour learning to tie a clove hitch, a figure eight, and a round turn with two half hitches.

"Okay, kids, that was fun!" Tornado said, clapping his hands for attention as if we were five-year-olds. "In case you were thinking I forgot — it's time to take a spin around the bay in my new boat." Tornado flashed his toothy smile and bowed. "It'll give you a taste of the pure pleasure of sailing and me a chance to show off." At least he'd gotten that last bit right.

All the kids bustled out of the building and followed Tornado down to the dock to where *The Princess* was moored. I tagged along at the end, waiting for my chance to duck out and head home early.

"You ever been sailing before?" a dark-haired boy asked me the moment I was about to run for it.

I shook my head.

"Me, neither," he said. "I've always wanted to, though."

I tried to slow my pace so I could be at the back by myself, but he just slowed his strides, too.

"It was my surprise gift just before my parents told me they were getting divorced this summer."

I felt a stab of pity. An embarrassing silence followed. I tried to think of something to say. "Well, at least you really wanted to take sailing lessons." By the way the conversation died, I realized I'd been kind of insulting. Fortunately, I didn't have time to feel bad.

"So here we are, class. Meet *The Princess*." Tornado grinned with pride as the students petted his gleaming white sailboat. All the brass fixtures sparkled in the sunlight, and the polished wood glowed. The sail was crisp white and fluttered in the breeze. And it was so big that even I felt overwhelmed by it. "Be careful not to scratch the wood or gum up the brass. Just keep your hands in your laps and sit back and enjoy. Today you're going to see a master sailor at work."

For the next hour we sailed around Mud Bay. I hadn't expected to be thrilled by the sensation of being pushed forward like a feather riding the breeze. And from out on the water I could almost make the houses disappear as I focused on the towering cedars. I didn't even mind watching Tornado, who stood at the helm like a Tarzan of the sea, with Melissa and Jennifer gazing up fondly on either side. To my relief the dark-haired boy had moved to the bow of the sailboat, where he hung over the rail like a happy dog with its head out the car window.

After *The Princess* docked and everyone was off, I felt as if my body was still swaying and lurching with the waves. I gripped the rail, afraid my legs would collapse.

Tornado gave his boat a little pat and let the sun gleam off his bright smile. "She's something, isn't she? Okay, then, next lesson you'll be spending time in your own sailboats." He pointed to a fleet of crummy old skiffs about six feet long. "You're going to learn about the rudder and how we use it to steer the boat."

When I started for home, I was actually skipping. Then I remembered I was still angry with my aunt, and I felt the simmering resentment return to the pit of my stomach.

As I walked through the front door, Aunt Margaret was in the kitchen pulling a pie out of the oven. "So how did it go? Was it fun? Did you meet anyone nice?"

"Oh, sure, I met two brainless, navel-gazing bubbleheads named Barbie One and Barbie Two! And let me see, who else? Oh, yeah, the instructor, who looks like a hot dog someone left on the barbecue too long and likes to be called Tornado. And then there was some kid whose parents just dumped the bad news on him that they're getting divorced."

I felt victorious as I watched my aunt's hopeful expression turn into one of disappointment. At that moment I heard the familiar sound of the screen swishing back and forth and dashed out to the porch.

"Hi, Eddy! What did I miss?" I scooted down the stairs and came to a halt at the edge of the mound of screened matrix.

"Oh, hello, Peggy. I was hoping I'd see you today. I discovered something very important and wanted to share it with you."

I followed Eddy over to the excavation pit and watched as she manoeuvered her body slowly and carefully inside it. She used her fine brush to clear the earth around a long bone before picking it up. I could see that the two ends were fragmented and cracked like a spent Roman candle on July 1. Eddy turned the ancient bone over, examining it from every angle as I waited patiently for her to tell me what was so interesting.

"Hmm ... this is a beauty, Peggy," she mumbled, holding the bone so she could peer through the hollow opening. "There it is. Take a look at these transverse lines in the shaft of this femur." She handed me the bone and told me to hold it up as if I were looking through a telescope. At first the centre was too narrow and dark to see anything, but then my eyes adjusted. "Now look carefully, Peggy. Hold it up so the light shines down through the shaft." Finally, my eyes focused on a fine net, almost like lace, spread across the inside of the bone not far from the midpoint. "Do you see it? It's almost like a spiderweb right there inside the bone."

I nodded.

"That's a transverse line, also known as a Harris line. It tells us at some point in this fellow's life — most likely early childhood — he experienced some kind of malnutrition. Probably there was a period when the village was short on food, like in late winter. Whatever the circumstances, they were serious enough to leave this type of scar inside his bones. He may even have been close to starving to death."

I gently handed the bone back to Eddy.

"Peggy, before there's any supper you have some chores to do." Aunt Margaret was standing at the top of the back stairs, her hands on her hips.

I flashed her my best glare and turned to Eddy. "I'm sorry I can't help you right now, Eddy. Aunt Deadly has other plans for me."

That night Aunt Margaret and I were at war. She said that I lacked discipline and gratitude and needed to help out more. Then she handed me a list of cleaning she wanted done. It was as if I were Cinderella and she had turned into my evil stepmother. All this fuss because I didn't tell her where I was going.

I dusted the living room, vacuumed the house, changed the kitty litter, emptied the dishwasher, and took the garbage out to the road — all without saying a word or even looking at her. Uncle Stuart flashed me a couple of smiles, but I could tell he wasn't going to get in the middle of the feud. As soon as we finished our very quiet supper, I ran up to my room and closed the door. If I'd had a DO NOT DISTURB sign, I'd have hung it on the doorknob. I flopped down on my bed, and started planning ways to get Aunt Margaret's goat.

I really wanted to work on my necklace, but I promised myself I wasn't going to say a word to my aunt all night, even if it meant not visiting Mrs. Hobbs.

I thought about calling Mom, but I knew I'd open up like a floodgate and tell her how miserable I was. Then she'd feel really bad and start to cry again, and then I'd feel worse than I already did.

After a while, I was exhausted at being angry, so I tried to remember what Eddy had said about transverse lines. I couldn't imagine a hunger so deep that it left scars on my bones. I remembered one time Mrs. Hobbs had talked about growing up during the Great Depression of the 1930s. It was a time when a lot of people were out of work and had to live on small food rations. I wondered if Mrs. Hobbs had transverse lines.

Except for the lapping of the waves on the beach, the village is quiet and still. Almost all the people are out fishing or gathering fruits from the small prairie behind the village. There is a familiar prickle of excitement as everyone works to gather and prepare the last of the winter food.

Strips of drying fish and deer meat hang from the rafters of the clan house. The beach is strewn with woven grass mats covered in sweet berries drying in the sun. And stacks of the oily olachen fish, threaded with wicks, are bundled and ready to light the nights when the long darkness comes.

Today the men and women are at the river's mouth. The water is so thick with bright red salmon that it looks like blood. The men catch the fish in their dip nets and throw them onto the shore where the women wait with their sharp clamshell knives. Many of the young people are out on the sand bars collecting clams and crabs for roasting. Only a few of the old women remain in the camp to keep the squawking gulls and ravens from stealing the berries and meat.

Shuksi'em sits outside the clan house. He has just finished the last of his duck soup with the tender inner bark of hemlock. Now he must return to his work. He pulls the heavy deerskin onto his lap. With his bone tool he scrapes the skin, wearing away the old flesh and softening the hide. The work is familiar and rhythmic. He rubs his stomach with its painful fullness from eating too much. It reminds him to thank the Great Spirit for the abundance of food this season. Not every year has been so good.

He recalls the pain of an empty stomach, long ago when he was a boy. The run of salmon had been small that summer, and winter came early and stayed long. For many weeks the tiny, cold, white stars piled higher and higher, making it difficult to leave the big house. The supply of food in the storage boxes was getting very low. Outside, the freezing winds lashed at the clan lodge, shaking the rafters and walls. Even the air inside was icy cold. Only a few of the men dared to go out to gather wood. Sometimes they managed to catch a rabbit or a seabird for a bit of fresh meat.

Many of the old and very young died that winter, their wasted bodies buried in the snow until melting time. No one spoke the names of the dead for fear their ghosts would return to haunt the living. Sleep, if it came, was the only escape from the misery of the gnawing hunger.

Shuksi'em now thinks of his baby sister. He recalls watching his mother, so weak herself, anxiously mash her tiny ration of dried fish and try pushing it into the baby's mouth, but the food would not stay down. Neither infant nor mother had the energy to cry.

The day his little sister's spirit left her body, sunshine began peeking through the clouds, and drops of melting snow started falling from the roof. But the great sun was too late to save his sister. Like so many of the children in their clan, he was scarred by his loss.

But Shuksi'em does not want to think about this for long. He rubs his full stomach again and returns to his work.

CHAPTER 7

The next day I got ready for sailing class before Aunt Margaret had a chance to tell me to. If she wanted me to be independent and disciplined, I would be — so much that she'd see I didn't need her. When I came downstairs, she greeted me as if nothing was wrong between us. She had made pancakes for breakfast, but I said I wasn't hungry. I lied. I was really hungry. Not so bad to get transverse lines in my bones, but enough that my stomach growled all the way to the sailing clubhouse. My aunt came to the door and waved goodbye, but I pretended not to see her.

I figured I could stay mad at Aunt Margaret for a very long time, especially when I thought about the exciting discoveries Eddy would make again that day without me. That morning I took the grassy trail that ran behind the houses. As I strolled along it, I noticed pop cans, snack bags, and bits of plastic. There was even an old tire. I wondered if one day future archaeologists would call these pieces of garbage artifacts. And if they did, what would this midden of modern waste say about the people of my time?

When I arrived at sailing class, Tornado had already assigned me a partner. We were to practise all our knots, especially the clove hitch.

"Your name's really Thorbert?" I said. "You're

kidding, right?" The moment after I said it I realized it was a pretty insensitive thing to say. The dark-haired kid from the day before was trying to introduce himself, and here I was insulting him again. Then I realized my face was twisted and pinched exactly the way Aunt Margaret's got when she disapproved of something.

"Yup, stupid, isn't it?" he said. I felt worse when his face turned a pale shade of pink. "My dad was on some Viking kick. He named me Thorbert and my younger brother Goran after some distant ancestor or something."

I was sorry for the kid. Why did parents do stuff like that? "So do people ever call you Thor or Bert?"

"Sometimes, but they both sound just as dorky."

I didn't say anything, but I thought so, too. "Well, at least it's distinctive. My mom named me Margaret after my aunt. It's a pretty stodgy, old-fashioned name, but at least no one calls me that."

I decided I liked Thorbert and nicknamed him TB. He didn't talk that much or ask a lot of questions about my mom and dad. And he was also pretty good at knots. Later Tornado assigned each pair of students a sailboat. Ours was called *The Busy Bee*. We learned to manoeuvre the rudder, set the sail, then trim the sail. At the end of class Tornado said TB and I were doing so well he wanted us to demonstrate mooring a skiff for the next lesson.

"Okay, kids, that's it for today. Tomorrow we're going to practise manoeuvring the rudder some more and learn some new things, too." Tornado winked and shot his used-car-salesman finger at everyone. "And like they say — be there or be …" He paused. "What's the rest of it?"

"Square!" shouted about five kids.

"Right, be there or be square." He flashed his toothpaste commercial smile and waved everyone off.

TB and I walked along McBride together. We talked for a while about his parents' breakup. I didn't feel like sharing that things weren't all that happy at my house, either, so I told him about the excavation in my backyard.

"So you're the kid who found the old bones. I heard about you from my neighbour. Must be kind of creepy having some dead guy in the backyard."

I couldn't help feeling a little annoyed that TB sounded like Aunt Margaret. "It's kind of hard to explain, but it doesn't feel creepy to me," I said, trying to be patient. "When I started helping with the excavation, I thought it would be really cool to dig up the old bones and artifacts. I thought it would be fun if I could help piece them together like a LEGO project or a jigsaw puzzle. But I've been learning that the bones can actually tell you something about the person." By the look on TB's face, I could tell he didn't really get it. "I know it sounds kind of weird, but I feel like I'm getting to know this guy. It's like I've been reading his diary, except it's bones and not words on paper."

When TB and I came to the corner of McBride and Sullivan, he turned north. "That neighbour you were talking about wouldn't happen to be Mrs. Hobbs, would it?" I asked.

TB grinned. "Yup, that's her. She's like the best neighbour anyone could have. She's always baking us pies and cookies."

I felt the sting of jealousy. Somehow I had always

imagined Mrs. Hobbs was just my special friend. "Yeah, and aren't her double chocolate chip cookies amazing?" I said. Just then I decided I'd stop by Mrs. Hobbs's house and say hello. When TB turned into his neat bungalow with its white picket fence and daisies nestled together in clumps, I waved goodbye and went on to Mrs. Hobbs's place one house down.

Before I even knocked at the door I heard her inside talking to Chester. "Oh, what a surprise," she said when she came to the door. "I was wondering when you were coming over again. Come in, dear."

"I can't right now, Mrs. Hobbs. My aunt's expecting me home soon. I just finished my sailing lesson. You know the kid next door, Thorbert? He's in my class. We're partners."

"Thorbert? Isn't that lovely. He's such a dear boy. With his parents divorcing and all, he can really use a good friend like you. But when did this all start?"

"After I was here the other night, my aunt told me I had to take sailing lessons. She said I had too much free time on my hands. She makes me feel like I'm in the army."

"Well, she's just trying her best to look after you, Peggy. It must be hard for her, too, you know."

I wasn't going to let Aunt Margaret off that easy, even if Mrs. Hobbs said so.

"All right now, how about that necklace of yours? If you can't come in now, how about coming after supper?"

I think I skipped all the way up Sullivan. When I was almost home, I remembered the long list of chores my aunt would have for me. If I stayed out of her way and worked hard, I could get everything done and still have time to spend with Mrs. Hobbs.

"You're home. Did you have a nice day?" my aunt asked when I came through the door.

I nodded as I went to the sink for a drink of water.

"Still not talking to me, are you?"

I knew I could outlast Aunt Margaret. And no matter how much she tried to get me to talk to her, I wouldn't. Then I remembered I wanted her permission to go out later and decided I'd better try to be nice.

"Well, if you won't talk to me, then you'd better go outside and talk to your friend, Dr. McKay."

I dashed over to the back door. "Eddy, you're still here. I thought you'd be gone by now. Did you find anything today?" I ran down the stairs, stopping excitedly by her side.

Eddy laughed and waved her hands at me as if she were trying to slow down a runaway horse. "Whoa, girl! I'm not still here. I only just got here."

"Great! That means I can still help you." I ran over to the pile of tools under the stairs and got the bucket, trowel, and dustpan. Eddy had already pulled back the tarp from the burial and bunched it over by the hydrangea bush.

"Yes, there's something quite amazing I noticed yesterday when I was finishing up. I wanted you to be the first to see it." Eddy used both her hands to pick up the ancient skull that had been resting right side down. When she turned it over, I saw a hole in the forehead shaped like a jelly bean.

"This is really exciting, Peggy — and important. I still need to examine this in the lab, but I'm pretty sure this hole in the frontal bone is a case of trephination!"

Her voice was kind of giddy, like mine when I was excited about something.

"A trephi ... what?" I asked.

"Trephination. That's the term for a primitive skull operation. It wasn't that common, and there are only a few dozen cases of prehistoric operations like this in the world. We believe it was done to relieve pressure on the brain caused possibly by an injury or illness."

Just the thought made me wince and rub my forehead.

"It's quite possible the case of mastoiditis we discovered may have caused an excess of fluid in the brain — quite painful I'd imagine. I need to record this before I do anything else, then follow up with some photographs. How about handing me a caliper from my tool kit?"

I picked up the small metal tool with its two curved needle-like pincers and gave it to her.

Eddy opened the caliper and began measuring the hole. She determined the width and length from inside the opening, then calculated the thickness of the bone and the area of bone that had healed. Finally, she filled out three data forms, writing lots of paragraphs and making tiny diagrams.

"How would they have cut an opening like this?" I asked, locked in a stare with the empty eye sockets below the hole. I wasn't sure I really wanted to know the answer.

"I imagine they used a very sharp stone blade, or maybe even the sharpened edge of a clamshell, to cut and scrape a small hole into the skull. It would've been a slow process, and there's nothing to indicate they had the means to numb the pain. Once the built-up fluid drained out, they would've covered the wound with some traditional plant medicine to help it heal."

All I could think of to say was "gross," but Eddy didn't seem to hear.

"There isn't a lot of information on these operations because they're so rare. But from what we know, most of the patients didn't survive. On the other hand, our friend here appears to have fared quite well."

"How can you tell, Eddy?"

"By looking at the rounding of the edges and the form of the hole, I can see there was a period of healing. The skin probably grew over, and there was even some new growth in the bone, though obviously not enough to close up the hole. At the moment everything I see tells me this fellow went on to live for quite a while."

Eddy placed the skull on the grass and laid her ruler beside it as a scale for size. Then she started taking photographs. As the camera shutter clicked rapidly, I stared at the small hole just big enough for a nickel to slip through.

On the beach below Shuksi'em, the men are piling the day's catch. A boy yanks the tail of a small woolly dog trying to make off with a fish almost the same size. Other children dance in the sand, shouting at the squawking seabirds hovering in the sky.

Soon the women come down to prepare the salmon. Each carries her own tools — a bone abrader for scraping scales and a flaked flint knife for gutting. Today's catch will be smoked and stored in the cache boxes for winter.

Shuksi'em can see that the days are getting shorter and feels the nights becoming cooler. He hates the damp cold.

He thinks this land would be paradise if it were not for the rain and many days of black clouds. These past few winters he would go for two or three weeks easily without so much as poking his head out from the clan house to see the sky.

He remembers one winter long ago that he thought would be his last. A terrible pain behind his ear moved up to his head and hurt so badly he thought he was caught in the jaws of a black bear. Then his uncle, the village healer, said he would cure his pain.

All his relatives and friends gathered in the big house and watched as the healer cut into his head. The scraping sound coming from the sharp stone blade made the inside of his head shiver. He can still remember Talusip's voice quavering as she and the other women chanted songs. Soon a black wall went up, and he slept for many days.

For a long time after that Shuksi'em was afraid to lie down. He worried that everything inside his head would fall out — his memories, thoughts, and fears lying on the dirt floor for all to see and trample on. For a long while the clan teased him about his hole, saying it was like the soft place on a new baby's head.

Now, many years after, his hair still has not grown over the spot. But at least the pain is gone.

Eddy and I worked for a long while. I hadn't noticed that the light had turned dim from the low marine clouds that had moved in from the Pacific Ocean. When we finally stopped for the night, the entire skeleton was exposed and sitting neatly on top of the dirt.

"I need to get some photographs of the entire burial, but the lighting isn't any good," Eddy said. "Let's just cover it up for the night and I'll take pictures in the morning. Once that's done, we'll be able to remove the bones and take them where they'll be safe."

"I can cover up the burial and put things away," I offered.

"That would be great, Peggy. I want to try to make it to the store before it closes and buy my grandson a birthday present. He's turning seven tomorrow."

I walked out front with Eddy and waited until her red truck rumbled to life and drove off down the street. When I returned to the backyard, I was alarmed to see my aunt's cat, Duff, inside the burial. "Duff, scoot! Get out of there!" I lunged at him, waving my arms at the same time. I startled him, and he darted out of the hole, glaring at me as he scampered up the stairs.

When I glanced back at the burial, I saw he had kicked up some of the dirt and pushed the skull from its resting place. "Stupid cat," I muttered. I could see how the speckled earth still formed a rounded indentation where it had cradled the skull and decided I should put the skull back in its original place. As I held it, I was surprised how heavy it was. I ran my hand over the smooth surface and let my fingers trace the edges of the eyes and the sharp and cracked bridge of the nose.

When I lowered the skull into the cup-shaped dirt, I noticed a small, perfectly round stone. It must have been buried in the soil until Duff had kicked it out of place. Gently, I put the skull down and picked up the round stone, ignoring my thumping heart. It was probably just an ordinary rock, I told myself.

The smooth black disc was a little larger than an Oreo cookie. But when I turned it over to study the other side, I almost dropped it. There, staring up at me, were the delicate features of a tiny face. Above the fine and gracefully carved face was a tiny hole drilled clear through to the other side. As I held the smooth stone in my hand and turned it over and over, the oil in my fingers deepened the gleam and the details of the face became clearer and even more stunning.

I imagined Eddy's reaction when she saw the tiny carving for the first time. Then I remembered what she'd said only last week: "It's the artifact in situ that tells you the most." As I gazed at the gleaming object, I hoped Duff and I hadn't destroyed too much information. Quickly, I returned it close to its original resting place. Just after I replaced the skull, I heard footsteps coming from behind.

"Hello, little Miss Archaeologist. Now what are you up to?"

Mr. Grimbal was standing behind me. Before I could retrieve the tarp and cover the excavation pit, he bent down and started jabbing at the bones and skull. My heart almost leaped into my throat as his hand got closer to the small carving underneath.

"I don't think you should be here," I said. "Eddy wouldn't like you touching the burial."

Mr. Grimbal didn't seem to take notice of me. He just grinned. "So what did she do with that nice little awl you found the other day? Bet the old biddy's already stuffed it in some dusty drawer at the museum, along with dozens of others just like it. Find anything else?"

I was afraid that Mr. Grimbal could read my mind.

"Oh, sure you did," he answered for me. "Burials like this usually have several things — stone and bone tools, trinkets, other stuff like that. Right? Of course, I'm right. So what else?"

I stared back at Mr. Grimbal, my brain in slow motion. "Are you here to speak to my Aunt Margaret? Because if you are, she's not going to sell anything. She doesn't even know about the artifacts we've found."

"Artifacts, eh? Well, at least I know now there's more than one." He smirked at me as if I were some dumb little kid he'd cheated. "Well, just to give you an idea about what some of those artifacts are worth, that little bone awl could fetch four or five hundred dollars from an avid collector. I bet you could use some money like that."

"No, I don't need any money, Mr. Grimbal." I decided to make a dive for the tarp and quickly spread it over the burial. At least it would stop him from fondling the skull.

"Then again, if you found something really unique, something rare, you could get several thousand dollars for it."

I turned my back on him and began placing the large rocks on the corners of the tarp. The wind had picked up, and the low grey clouds above seemed dark and dangerous. Why was he here now, just after I discovered the delicate little carving? Maybe he really could read my mind. I stole a quick glance at his face and shuddered at his grimacing smile.

Just then Aunt Margaret's voice shot out the kitchen window like a bolt of lightning from the clouds above. "Peggy, it's time to come in. After you've scrubbed yourself spotless, you can reheat your supper in the microwave." At that moment I couldn't have been happier to hear my aunt's bossy command.

"Think about what I said, kid. There must be

something you want. Everyone needs money, right?" Then Mr. Grimbal turned and sauntered slowly out of the yard.

I bolted the gate and leaned Uncle Stuart's shovel against it as heavy raindrops began to fall. Quickly, I ran around the yard and put away all the tools. By the time I finished, I was nearly soaked through. But before dashing into the house I hesitated. I looked at the tarp-covered burial for the last time and shivered at the thought of Mr. Grimbal sneaking in and stealing the little carving. With one swift movement I ripped back the plastic and rolled the skull over. In near darkness with rain already forming pools of water, I fingered the coarse earth until I found the small stone. I grabbed it firmly and pushed it deep into my pant pocket.

Minutes later, when I placed my dinner in the microwave oven, my hands were still shaking. When the timer beeped, my heart skipped and my hand automatically flew to my side to check for the small hard lump. I took out the plate of spaghetti with tofu meatballs — Uncle Stuart's specialty — and headed up to my room to eat. Besides finding a safe place to hide the stone carving, I wanted to search on the Internet for information about Coast Salish art. I also needed to decide what to tell Eddy.

"Where are you going with that?" Aunt Margaret demanded. "You know the rule in our house — all food is eaten in the kitchen." She pointed to a chair.

My heart sank, and I flopped down on the seat.

"Peggy, did you wash your hands? It certainly doesn't look like you did."

I glanced down at my hands and the caked dirt under

my fingernails. Shuffling over to the sink, I turned on the tap. When I finished washing, I sat down and started gobbling my food as fast as possible.

"Slow down or you'll choke," Aunt Margaret cautioned. "Why the glum look? I thought you'd be happy after spending the evening digging up bones with your friend."

Just then my fork dropped out of my hand and clattered onto the plate. "Oh, my gosh, Mrs. Hobbs!"

"What about her?" my aunt asked.

"She invited me to spend the evening with her. We're making something — a surprise for Mom. Aunt Margaret, I've got to run over to her house and apologize."

"Now? Peggy, it's too late in the evening to go knocking on someone's door. And even if you had her telephone number, it wouldn't be polite to call. She's probably already in her pajamas and ready for bed. You'll just have to go see her after your sailing class tomorrow."

"Please, Aunt Margaret, it'll only take fifteen minutes. I'll run all the way there and all the way back."

"I can see you're upset, but not tonight, Peggy. I've already explained that it's too late to be calling on people."

"But —"

"Peggy, stop. I said no. Maybe your mother lets you argue back, but I won't have it. Now finish your meal and then it's time for you to get ready for bed."

I pushed back the chair and stomped out of the kitchen. I knew if I stayed there another minute I wouldn't be able to control what I said or did.

"What about your supper?" my aunt called after me.

I ran into my room and slammed the door. Aunt Margaret was so unfair, and she always treated me like a little kid. No matter how long I lived with her things would never be any different.

"I've got to get away from here," I growled out loud. "I don't care what Mom says. I'm not going to live with Aunt Margaret anymore." I turned over and buried my face in my pillow to stop myself from crying. Everything in my head was swirling around madly — visions of Mrs. Hobbs waiting for me, my aunt barking orders, Mr. Grimbal smirking. Then I remembered the little carved face I'd found less than an hour before. I pulled it from my pocket. As I held it between my thumb and forefinger, I wondered about the small hole at the top. It reminded me of the hole in the skull Eddy had shown me earlier. At that moment I realized the little carving was a pendant.

I imagined a leather string bearing the little face. Maybe the necklace had been around the man's neck when he was buried. Did men wear necklaces back then? He was a carver. Did he make it himself? Or was it a gift?

Soon I was enveloped by a wave of exhaustion and felt myself slipping down a dark hole like Alice in Wonderland chasing after the rabbit. I tucked the small carved stone under my pillow and closed my eyes.

Shuksi'em is surprised how well his hands feel today. He is glad, for this is the day he begins carving with the black stone. Carefully, he removes the fragile slate-like rock from the wet deerskin. His fingers tingle with excitement, for this strange new thing is just what he desired for the gift he is making for Sleek Seal, his granddaughter. He studies the grain in the stone. Shuksi'em must first see the carving in his mind and then he will know where to make the cuts. The Chinook told him the stone came from far away, over the mountains and past the sea. They said that the people of the stone called it Kwawhlhal. Shuksi'em thinks it a strange word indeed. He traded a deerskin and many dried salmon to obtain the stone. But he does not mind. It is a small price to pay for such a jewel.

The stone is soft, and Shuksi'em must be careful as he carves. He is using his best shell knife to scrape at the course edges, slowly smoothing and rounding them. The vision in his mind grows clearer as the stone begins to take form. This small amulet will hang around the neck of his granddaughter, who is soon to have her passage to womanhood ceremony. Shuksi'em wills the protecting spirit to enter this gift with each careful stroke.

Though he must not speak of it, Sleek Seal is his special granddaughter. Shuksi'em sees in her the best of his people. He laughs inside as he thinks how often she surpasses her brothers at catching fish from the shore. Or how clever she is with hunting the small animals close to camp. No one taught her these things — for girls were not made for such work — but she always watches her uncles carefully and learns.

Even more unusual are Sleek Seal's stories. Many times in a day the young ones ask her to tell them tales. Some are the ones she has heard from him. But others are not familiar to their village. They come from inside her.

Shuksi'em remembers when Sleek Seal reached her ninth summer. The women turned her attention to new tasks. She was quick to learn their work — making flour from fern roots, weaving spruce roots tight enough to hold water, fashioning string from nettle fibres and knives from mussel shells. Now she is very clever at making her own clothing of cedar bark, skins, and fur. And her aunts are very surprised at how easily she can beach a canoe without getting wet.

But no matter how busy the women keep her, Sleek Seal finds moments to slip away to visit her grandfather. And at night she never misses his stories.

Now Shuksi'em labours greatly over his gift. He wants its power to protect his young granddaughter who has been made an offer of marriage by a young man from another village. If her parents accept the offer at the fall clan gathering, Sleek Seal will leave her family's clan house to join his. She has objected to the match, but the matter is not up to her. Though this granddaughter is in her thirteenth summer, Shuksi'em thinks she may not be ready. He has spoken to the girl's father, who promises to consider the proposal carefully.

Nevertheless, Sleek Seal's passage ceremony will take place soon, and she is preparing for the dances. Shuksi'em will make sure the pendant is ready. Besides having protective powers, it must be beautiful. When his work is complete, he will take it to the shaman for a blessing.

"Hello, Grandfather," comes the sweet, familiar voice from behind.

Shuksi'em manages to slip the precious stone and his carving knife under his cedar blanket quickly.

"I've brought you some of the fresh salmon berries you like so much." Sleek Seal says, placing the small wooden bowl filled with the delicious pink pearls into her grandfather's lap. Gently, she slides herself close to his side and pulls from her leather pouch a ball of matted hairs from the woolly *dog. She plucks at the fine hairs, then begins twining them into long, soft strings. The two sit silently side by side, happy in each other's company.*

CHAPTER 8

I woke early to the sound of fat raindrops pelting against my window. I couldn't go back to sleep because the resentment I'd gone to bed with the night before was still there, filling me with a darkness blacker than the clouds outside. So I stayed in bed, feeling tense and raw, wishing as never before that I was far away from here and back with my mother.

The phone rang, and I waited for my aunt to answer it. I was afraid I'd sent thought waves to my mom and now she was calling. I knew if I talked to her she'd hear something in my voice and start asking questions.

I tensed when I heard my aunt cross the hall and open my bedroom door.

"Peggy, that was the sailing instructor on the phone. He says it's too stormy for sailing today and cancelled the lesson."

My hands relaxed, but I didn't say anything to Aunt Margaret. I turned over in my bed and heard her quietly back out of the room and shut the door.

When I decided to get up and dress, I opened the top drawer and was surprised to see rows of clean, paired socks. The other drawers were full of neat piles of pants and T-shirts, too. I remembered taking the large mound of dirty clothes down to the laundry room the other day, but never gave any thought as to how it would get clean and back in my drawers. Now everything I owned was tidy and folded — just the way my aunt liked it. I pulled everything out and mixed it all up, then stuffed the heap back into the drawers.

I decided to go over to Mrs. Hobbs's house first thing and explain about the night before. I hoped she wouldn't feel disappointed with me. I wondered if I should tell her about finding the ancient pendant and Mr. Grimbal's sudden visit — and the big fight I'd had with Aunt Margaret. Maybe if she knew how unhappy I was she'd invite me to stay with her.

As I slipped into my clothes, I had visions of Mrs. Hobbs adopting me as her granddaughter. We could collect shells together and make necklaces. And she'd always bake double chocolate chip cookies and berry pies for me. And I would live happily ever after. "Right!" I said out loud as I snapped myself out of the daydream. "Things never work out that well for you."

When I entered the kitchen, I heard my aunt's and uncle's hushed voices coming from the living room. I pulled on my old windbreaker and quietly slipped out the back door. When I stepped out into the chilly wind and steady drizzle of rain, I realized my worn-out jacket wouldn't keep me warm. But there was no way I was going back inside the house.

As I walked down Kidd Street and over to Agar, I felt as if I were wandering through a ghost town. All the streets were deserted, and even the gulls were nowhere to be seen. I tucked my arms close around me and ducked my head low. When I got to Mrs. Hobbs's front door, there were no warm smells of fresh cookies or a kindly voice talking to Chester. I rang the doorbell twice and heard it echo inside the house. When there was no answer, I tried pounding the door with my fist.

After waiting a long time, I walked back out to the road and headed toward Blackie's Spit, even though the storm was now whipping at the trees and rattling windows. I knew it was unlikely, but I still hoped I'd find her out on the sandbars looking for shells, with Chester waddling behind. When I reached the end of the narrow finger of land, I wasn't surprised that no one was around. I turned back into the full force of the cold wind. For a few moments I opened my jacket and held my arms out wide to see if the gale would lift me into the sky like a kite — an unanchored kite tossed around the atmosphere, being pulled farther and farther from Earth.

With nowhere else to go, I went back home. When I came into the kitchen, I noticed a book sitting on the table. A wild, stunning wolf on the cover jumped off the jacket at me. I read the words framing the eerie mask: *Cultures of the North Pacific Coast* by Philip Drucker. It was an old book, worn at the corners, and many of the pages had been dog-eared with pencilled notes in the margin.

"Peggy, have you been out wandering around in this storm?" Aunt Margaret gasped when she came into the kitchen. "I thought you were still upstairs in bed sleeping." Then she noticed me staring at the book on the table. "Dr. McKay dropped that off for you. She thought you might be interested in looking at it."

"Did she say anything else?"

"Not much, just that she'd wait until the weather improved to come back and finish the excavation. Do you feel better now that you've had a chance to speak to Mrs. Hobbs?"

"She wasn't home," I said without looking up from the book.

"That's too bad, but I'm sure she'll understand when you get a chance to explain."

"Yeah, you're right. She'll understand because she gets me." I avoided my aunt's hurt expression and opened the book to the index in the back. There was a long list of references to the Coast Salish, like dance ceremonies, kinship structures, potlatches. I flipped to the section on potlatches. I already knew that the word meant *gift* and that they were traditional gatherings where people of different villages came together for days of ceremonies and feasting to honour someone who died or a chief who wanted his status to be recognized. I always thought it was cool that the true sign of a wealthy chief was not how much he had but how much he could afford to give away.

Under my breath I read: "Some Coast Salish were fond of the 'scramble' as a method of distributing goods to commoners, but never to chiefs." I imagined men, women, and children playfully racing around to gather bone fish hooks, awls, and baskets to take home. I riffled through more pages to see what other things I could learn about potlatches. I skimmed over the subheadings: "The Formalities of Potlatches," "The Potlatch and Loans of Interest," "Rivalry Potlatches." The last title caught my attention. I read the first line of the paragraph: "The spectacular rivalry potlatches were all to humiliate a rival." That was when I remembered Aunt Margaret was still there staring at me.

"Peggy, I'd like to talk with you." She nervously cleared her throat. "I realize you've been unhappy. It's natural that you want to be with your mom. But the fact is she can't care for you right now. I know she wants to, but if she's going to get on her feet she needs to —"

"Make sure I'm out of the way, right?" I interrupted.

"That's not what I was going to say."

"No, but you were thinking it."

"No, I wasn't!"

I hadn't noticed before, but my aunt's face was all pink and puffy.

"Look, Peggy, I admit you haven't exactly been a joy to have around. But I know it's because your life is all upside down. I also admit that I'm strict and —"

"Unreasonable? Demanding? Unfair?" I fired back.

"Okay, maybe there have been times when that was true. But then you've been disobedient, irresponsible, ungrateful, unforgiving, cold, and secretive."

My aunt's words were like blows to my head and stomach. Now her face was glowing red, and her eyes were moist.

"I promised your mom that I'd look after you. And that's what I want to do. But if this is going to work you need to cooperate ... and show respect."

"Mom always taught me that respect is a two-way street, Aunt Margaret," I spat back.

"That's true, but sometimes parents know what's best and the child just needs to trust and be obedient."

I felt as if an explosion had gone off inside my head. "Parents? You're not my parents and you never will be. My real mom loves me no matter what I wear or say or do. But you'll never think I'm good enough. You don't like my clothes, my hair isn't combed enough,

I don't sit straight enough. How do you think it feels living with someone who picks at every thing you do?" When the words stopped shooting out of my mouth, Aunt Margaret covered her tear-streaked face with her hands and left the kitchen.

I ran upstairs and accidentally kicked Duff, who was sitting in the middle of the landing. *"Yeowwww!"* he screeched.

"Shut up!" I cursed, and was glad I'd kicked him.

There was only one person in the world who really cared about me. And if I wanted to be with her, we'd need money. I reached under the pillow and found the smooth little disc. Without glancing at its tiny face, I put it in my pocket and dumped Eddy's book onto the bed.

Outside, the rain had slowed to a sprinkle. When I marched as far as Beecher Street, I felt calmer. I decided to stop and catch my breath in Heron Park and think about what I was going to do next. I'd passed by the little park at the entrance of Crescent Beach many times but had never walked through it before. In the middle of the park was a huge rock deposited in the last ice age, a stinging reminder of my insignificant existence. As I followed the little path that led around the boulder, I spotted a bronze plaque. It read: "These petroglyph symbols were carved into this rock by the prehistoric inhabitants of this area."

Glancing up, I saw some indentations in the rock. I ran my hand over the rough surface to feel the deep groves. Then I stepped back several feet to see the design. It was a simple pattern of circles and dots. As I studied the petroglyphs, they began to look like the faces of skinny, bulgy-eyed aliens.

Before coming to Crescent Beach I'd never heard of the Coast Salish. Now, everywhere I went, I found reminders of their existence. I wondered what the picture meant and wished I could ask Eddy, but I knew after today I'd never be able to look her in the eye again.

I dragged my feet slowly along the sidewalk, passing Sunshine Organic Grocery and Tong's Eatery. When I went by the Beecher Street Café, I noticed Bob Puddifoot inside, pushing a large muffin into his mouth and then gulping from a tall coffee mug.

Finally, I reached the old grey building with the sign that read: REAL TREASURES AND GIFTS. In the lower left corner of the window was another sign: WANTED: NATIVE ARTIFACTS. WILL PAY TOP DOLLAR.

My stomach knotted up and my shoulders tensed as I peered through the dusty window. I'd never been inside Mr. Grimbal's store, and I almost hoped the place was closed. But when I pulled on the handle the door easily swung open.

Right inside the entrance stood two large totem poles that reached to the ceiling. They looked like stoic sentinels guarding the entry. At the top of one was some kind of bird — an eagle or hawk, I guessed. In its talons was a killer whale. And below it was a bear, or maybe it was a wolf. I wasn't sure. But it was the other pole that really caught my attention. At the very bottom was a human child clutched by a figure with an eerie black face, big red lips, and eyes that were dark and empty.

"Don't be afraid of Tsonokwa ... she won't bite you. Not right now, anyway."

I spun around and saw Mr. Grimbal laughing at me with his raspy voice, which turned into a sputtering cough. He was behind a glass counter grinning his yellowy smile. In his hand he held an oddly shaped pipe that billowed tiny clouds of smoke. My insides felt all twisted, but I ignored the fear. Carefully, I passed the fierce face on the totem pole and approached the counter, forcing a smile. "What did you call her, Mr. Grimbal? Was it Sonaka?"

"Close. Her name's Tsonokwa. She's the wild woman of the forest. All Native people had someone like her. The Coast Salish had a flying giantess called Quamichan, who liked to snack on juicy little children. Both Tsonokwa and Quamichan were mythical creatures useful to parents who wanted to frighten their children from straying far from home."

"Kind of like the bogeyman," I said.

"Yup, that's pretty much it." Mr. Grimbal took a long drag on his pipe and studied me intently. "So are you here to buy or sell?"

I blushed under his intimidating stare but didn't answer the question. Instead I looked around the shop. It was dusty, and the shelves were cluttered with a hodgepodge of souvenirs, books, and beach toys. Behind the glass counter, out of reach, were shelves full of what appeared to be Native artifacts.

I recognized several of the stone and bone objects. Some were just like the artifacts Eddy and I had found in our burial. There was a stone bowl with very thick sides, a large stone spool with a pointy tip, several burins, and two wooden rattles with carved killer whales. Then I saw a small carved figure that seemed to be made of the same gleaming black stone as the one I had tucked into my pocket.

Mr. Grimbal snickered. "Still got Miss Know-It-All running around your backyard?"

His voice had startled me from my thoughts. "She hasn't, I mean, we haven't finished the excavation. But it won't be long now." I needed to change the subject. "Do you know what the petroglyphs in Heron Park are about?"

"I do. What's it worth to you?" He snickered again, and I remembered what Eddy had said about Mr. Grimbal being a pirate and a grave robber.

"Just pulling your leg, kid." As he spoke, small puffs of smoke escaped from his mouth. "This place was once the summer village for the ancient ones. If you think it's nice now, back then it must have been a paradise." The usual harsh look on Mr. Grimbal's face softened. "This place had an abundance of food that kept those folks coming back every summer for thousands of years. But while they were gone for the winter they needed someone to watch over the place. I think those petroglyphs represented the spirits that guarded their fishing grounds, and when the people returned every spring, they were like the Welcome Wagon ladies."

He stopped and banged his pipe into an ashtray. That was when I realized that the grey stone pipe was actually a carving of a crouching wolf. It looked old.

"So that's what I think those petroglyphs are about. But don't take my word for it. Ask the good doctor what she thinks."

He took another long drag on his pipe and stared at me. I felt as if he were trying to size me up, so I looked down at the jewellery in the glass case.

"Of course, it doesn't take a Ph.D. to realize that

nature was important in the development of Native art. And this place had lots to work with — wildlife, mountains, the ocean. Even the sun and the moon." Mr. Grimbal pulled out a small silver pendant from the jewellery case. I peered at the etched design of a moon face — it had wide ovoid eyes and a u-form mouth.

"Did the ancient ones always carve from silver?" I asked.

"Not at all. Silver didn't come until much later. The first people would've carved from bone or stone."

Just then I felt a strong urge to check my pocket for the small stone carving. "What's that black stone there?" I asked, pointing at the shiny animal figure I'd seen when I first came into the store. Mr. Grimbal took the gleaming piece off the shelf. I touched the familiar cool, smooth surface.

"This is made of argillite. I got this little piece from a fellow who worked in Haida Gwaii — that's the Queen Charlotte Islands. He got it off some guy who needed cash to buy new fishing gear. But it's not that old, maybe a couple of hundred years."

I noticed the price tag said three thousand dollars. My palms suddenly became sweaty. I glanced around the store at the objects on the shelves. "Is it legal to buy artifacts, Mr. Grimbal?"

He was annoyed by my question. "It's not a black-and-white issue, kid. If you were walking along the sidewalk and found a diamond ring and had no idea who its owner was, wouldn't you keep it?"

"I'd try to find its owner first. Maybe place an ad in the paper."

"Well, what if its original owner was dead? That

would make it yours, and you could do whatever you wanted with it. You could wear it, give it away, sell it."

I felt Mr. Grimbal's eyes piercing through me, so I looked up at a framed newspaper article on the wall. The headline read: "Archaeologists Find Crescent Beach's Double Burial Romantic."

"What was that all about?" I asked, changing the subject again.

Mr. Grimbal rubbed his chin as if I were a mystery he was trying to figure out. "Back in the 1970s some fellows were making repairs to a burst water pipe. That's when they accidentally discovered the remains of some poor Indian and his woman. Their bones were all mixed together like they'd been embracing each other at the moment of death. All around them were arrowheads — some embedded in the ribs and skulls. It didn't take a bunch of experts to figure out those two died a violent death." Mr. Grimbal swiped his index finger across his throat. "But what made this story really interesting was how the burial was discovered on February 14 — St. Valentine's Day!"

A chill spread up my arms, leaving a trail of prickly goose bumps.

"Okay, kid, that's enough history lessons for today. I'm a busy man, and I'm pretty sure you've come to do business. So let's get to it."

His sudden confrontation launched my heart into my throat again. Nervously, I dug into my pocket for the stone pendant. I heard Eddy's voice in my head telling me to turn around and run. But then I thought about my mom and Aunt Margaret. At that moment it didn't take much for me to force myself to reason like

Mr. Grimbal — finders keepers — and that meant the pendant was mine.

I opened my sweaty palm and lifted it closer to Mr. Grimbal. He reached out to take it, and I quickly pulled my hand back.

"Well, I'm going to need a good look at it," he said.

"I'm not saying I'm going to sell it to you. I'm just wondering what you'd pay for an artifact like this." I'd have to be careful. This thing was the only chance for Mom and me.

Mr. Grimbal smirked. "Well, now, if that came from the burial in your yard, that would make it at least a couple of thousand years old. It's a pretty little thing, too." He rubbed his chin again, calculating something in his mind. "I could give you five hundred cash right now."

Blood rushed to my face, and I stuffed the stone back into my pocket and turned toward the door.

"Now don't rush off. If you're really serious about selling that thing, I could probably give you a better deal."

Mr. Grimbal wore a poker face, and I had no idea what he was thinking. "I want three thousand dollars," I told him. "It's that or no deal." I knew it was me talking, but I hardly recognized my own voice.

"Three thousand dollars? You've got to be kidding. No one in their right mind would pay that much. But seeing that I'm in a good mood today, I'll give you half that."

If I even hesitated, I knew he'd win. By now I had a pretty good idea what my artifact was worth, so I turned and walked quickly past Tsonokwa and out the door. As I moved up the sidewalk, Mr. Grimbal yelled at me from the door.

"Okay, okay, you've got a deal. Come back in an hour and I'll have the cash."

I tore up Beecher, passed the petroglyphs, and turned left on Sullivan. I didn't slow down until I knew I was out of Mr. Grimbal's sight. That was when I first felt the prickle of guilt as I thought about Eddy again. But she didn't know anything about the little carving. I reasoned that the old man in the burial had no use for it, while Mom and I really needed the money.

I ran into the backyard and bolted up the back stairs, avoiding the form under the orange tarp. I wanted to call Mom and tell her I'd won some money in a contest. What kind of a contest? I'd have to think first.

As I reached for the phone, I heard a knock at the front door. Then Uncle Stuart called out to my aunt. "Is Peggy back yet? There's someone here to see her."

Immediately, I knew it was Mrs. Hobbs and rushed down the hall. Before I got to the front door I saw Chester's nose sniffing just inside the doorway. I bent down and rubbed his head, but when I glanced up it wasn't Mrs. Hobbs standing behind him. It was TB. I frowned in disappointment.

"Hi, TB. What are you doing here ... with Chester?"

"I'm looking after him. I came over because I thought you'd want to know that Mrs. Hobbs was taken by ambulance to Peace Arch Hospital early this morning."

Did someone just slam me in the face with a frying pan? "She's sick? She's gone to the hospital?" My ankles melted, and I was afraid I'd collapse into a heap.

I felt my aunt place her hands on my shoulders,

which seemed to help steady me. "Hi, I'm Peggy's aunt. I heard you tell Peggy that Mrs. Hobbs is in the hospital. Thank you for taking the time to come here to tell her." Then she looked into my face. "We can go there right now if you want."

I was in a daze, but somehow I managed to nod.

CHAPTER 9

As Aunt Margaret and I drove up Crescent Road's windy hill, I caught glimpses of the grassy shoreline that gave way to the horseshoe-shaped bay below. If I looked beyond the houses and telephone wires, I could pretend I was seeing it as it was thousands of years ago.

When we got to the hospital, we found Mrs. Hobbs in room 316. The gloomy space was divided into quarters by curtains and was shared by three other elderly ladies. As I approached Mrs. Hobbs's bed, her eyes were closed and I noticed that her skin was pallid. Her silver hair, which was usually twisted into a neat bun at the back of her head, hung flat and lifeless around her face. She had clear plastic tubes in her nose, and a loud whirr came from the oxygen machine on the floor next to her. I think she must have sensed our presence, because she slowly opened her eyes.

"Oh, Peggy dear, how kind of you to come."

Kind? How could she say that? Last night I'd forgotten all about her. I'd probably caused her to get sick, too. I could feel my aunt close beside me, and at that moment I almost wanted to bury myself in her arms.

"Now don't be alarmed, honey," Mrs. Hobbs said. "I don't know what came over me, but I'll be fine soon." She closed her eyes, and at first I thought she'd drifted off to sleep. "Now I want you to go ahead and finish your mom's present. TB's mother has a key to my place. You go in and get that box of shells. It's still on top of the china hutch. Oh, and give dear old Chester a hug for me, will you?"

I jammed my palms into my eyes, pushing back the tears.

We didn't stay long. Aunt Margaret said Mrs. Hobbs needed to rest. The drive home was too quiet, so I turned on the radio. Immediately, the car was filled with the gentle strumming of a guitar and the sad twang of a country singer.

> You broke my heart when you left me all alone.
> No one to hug at night, or talk to on the phone.
> For months I prayed to God in heaven above,
> To give me strength to find new love.
> To give me strength to find new love.

I punched at the station tuner — a news bulletin about a car bomb somewhere in the Middle East. I punched it again — a commercial for life insurance. Finally, I snapped off the radio and sat quietly until we got back to Crescent Beach.

"I'd like to take a walk," I said when we passed the WELCOME TO CRESCENT BEACH sign.

Aunt Margaret pulled the car off to the side of the road. "It's been a very emotional day, Peggy. I'm not sure it's a good idea for you to be alone."

I was too tired to argue, so I just stared out the window.

"But if that's what you think you need, then I'll see you at home in a while."

"Thanks, Aunt Margaret." I got out of the car and watched as she drove off. Then I looked down Beecher Street. It was getting late, and I wondered if Mr. Grimbal was still waiting for me.

"We met with the women from the next village on the shores today," Talusip announces with a touch of annoyance in her voice. "They were gathering the sour apples from the beach. I told them it was too soon, but they did not listen." She rolls her roundness onto the bear rug beside her husband, but she is not ready to sleep. "They talked of the fall feast. They say their clan has many young women who will be honoured for their passage. I told them our Sleek Seal would be celebrated also. I told them how she will be adorned with a new deerskin dress trimmed with seal fur and how her chest will shimmer with a shell necklace fit for a princess." Talusip takes a deep breath. "Then that sour old Qulama said that Hulutin's family is sure to make an offer for him to marry her granddaughter. Aeiyyyy!" At this she is so angry that she rolls from bed and goes to their family fire to stir the hot coals.

Shuksi'em knows what is expected. He pushes himself up and pulls the fur blanket around him for warmth. "Perhaps this is a good thing. I have been thinking that it may be too soon for Sleek Seal to be given for marriage."

The bright flames of fire are small compared to the glare in Talusip's eyes. "I do not believe you are so slow-witted, old man. Do you forget? I was the same age when we were married so long ago. You did not seem to mind then. No, the time is right, and if Hulutin is to have a wife we must make sure that it is Sleek Seal." She gazes into the fire, commanding it to show her a plan that will secure her granddaughter's place.

Shuksi'em feels amused with his angry wife. "You are quite right, Wife. I must lie down and give the matter some serious thought." He lowers himself to his bed, careful not to chuckle too loudly, and soon falls asleep.

When I opened the shop door this time, I walked briskly past the totem poles, avoiding the dark face staring up at me.

"I was wondering if you'd changed your mind," Mr. Grimbal growled. "That wouldn't have been good, because I've already got someone interested in buying your carving."

Cautiously, I placed the pendant on the glass counter. Mr. Grimbal slid a white envelope across to me and snatched up the tiny face. "Oh, my! She's lovely." As he spoke, he looked so ... what?

Was it tenderness I saw? Admiration? Awe?

"I've never seen anything like it," he whispered. "After all this time, the skilfully crafted features are still so perfectly graceful. My goodness, this will make quite an addition to someone's collection."

I remembered what Mrs. Hobbs had said about the artifacts from Crescent Beach. Her words played over in my mind: "If they can't stay in the ground with their original owners, then they belong in a museum where everyone can enjoy them." More than anything I wanted to be with my mom. But if I sold the ancient stone carving, would Mrs. Hobbs's words haunt me forever? Could I be happy knowing I'd betrayed her and Eddy?

"Mr. Grimbal, I think I've changed my mind," I blurted.

Suddenly, all the kindness I'd seen in his face moments before disappeared and he glared down at me. "Don't tell me you want more money! Because that's all you're getting."

"No, that's not what I mean. I don't want to sell at all."

He clenched his fist firmly around the pendant and shoved the envelope with the money closer. "Too late. The deal's done." Then he wagged his finger at me. "And if you know what's good for you, you'll keep your mouth shut about this business." He turned and disappeared into another room. "Be careful of Tsonokwa on your way out." Then I heard his hideous laugh.

At that moment I didn't know who I hated more — Mr. Grimbal or myself. I picked up the bulging envelope filled with cash and tried to stuff it into my pocket, but it wouldn't fit. So I clasped it tightly in my hands and left the store.

When I got to Kidd Street and saw Eddy's red truck parked in front of the house, I groaned. I turned and walked up Sullivan instead, passing the park and the fish and chip shop. As I went by the large metal garbage bin, I noticed a long brown tail wagging behind it.

"Chester, what are you doing here?" The old beagle looked up for a moment, wagged his tail, then went back to sniffing, licking, and munching. I grabbed him by the collar and led him up the road.

When TB opened the front door, he grinned at the escapee I'd brought him. "Don't tell me — he was at the fish and chip shop, right?"

I scratched Chester behind the ears, then pushed him into the house.

"This is like the third time he's done that today." TB stepped out and closed the door. "So how's Mrs. Hobbs?"

"I don't know. She didn't look like herself, but she tried acting all cheerful and said she'd be fine."

"I hope so," TB said as large droplets of rain landed on my head. "Want to come in?"

"Thanks, but I'm not good company right now." I was going to say goodbye, but then I remembered what Mrs. Hobbs had said about the shells. "Mrs. Hobbs told me I could get her box of shells. Do you think you could let me into her house?"

"Sure, I'll get the key." A few minutes later we were inside Mrs. Hobbs's house. There was none of the familiar hominess I'd felt in the past. Without her the place felt empty. The metal tackle box was on the hutch where she'd said it would be.

I said goodbye to TB and headed toward the beach trail at the end of Sullivan. I walked until I came to the park bench tucked under the old willow. There was a small dry spot on the seat. Before sitting, I read the little brass sign embedded in the wood: IN LOVING MEMORY OF EUNICE BROWN — WONDERFUL MOTHER AND FRIEND.

I sat for a long time watching the nearly black waves wash in and out. As I thought about how the clouds and rain mirrored all the darkness I felt inside, I opened Mrs. Hobbs's shell box. On top was a small package wrapped neatly in newspaper and decorated with a pink bow. Written in ink were the words: "To Peggy." I replaced the gift with the fat envelope filled with cash.

My cheeks burned as I untied the ribbon and unfolded the paper. I immediately recognized the dozens of spiral snake-skinned shells strung together as *Ophiodermella cancellata* — the first shell Mrs. Hobbs had ever given me for my collection. Dangling like a pendant in the middle was a ridged whelk — Mrs. Hobbs's favourite shell. I breathed deeply before slipping it over my head.

That night I was surprised when Aunt Margaret let me eat my supper alone in my room. I told her I was going to work until I finished my shell necklace for Mom. I wanted to show Mrs. Hobbs when I went to visit her in the morning.

I was completely exhausted when I went to bed, but it was still hard to sleep. My mind kept replaying the events of the day. Every time I shut my eyes I saw Mrs. Hobbs all pale and lying in the hospital bed, and Mr. Grimbal snatching away the tiny carved face and laughing at me.

I guess I did fall asleep, because sometime in the night I had a nightmare — my aunt kicked me out of her house and I had to live in Mr. Grimbal's store with Tsonokwa, the evil hag who ate kids. The really scary part was when Tsonokwa chased me. As I was running away, I fell into the excavation pit, collapsing right into the bony arms of the old man. I think I yelled and woke myself up. After that I sat up in bed and stared into the darkness, refusing to go to sleep.

The days of the fall feast are nearly upon them, and the villagers work long hours preparing for the special occasion. Every family drags out their bear rugs to air them and bang the dirt and dust out. All the cedar bedding is dumped in the woods, and fresh boughs are cut. Now the big house smells like a forest.

Piled in the corner are stacks of gifts for the visitors — deerskins, rabbit pelts, dried salmon, spears, fishing nets. The children have been collecting the large unbroken clam-shells for the guests to use for their food and drink. When the women finish packing the storage boxes, the men lower them into the cool cache pits.

While everyone is busy, Shuksi'em hobbles down the beach, far from the clan. He is glad no one notices him leave. He has only a short time left to finish his gift for Sleek Seal. Sitting on the warm sand, he unties his leather pouch hanging from his cedar bark garment. Carefully, he opens the bag and removes his good carving tools. Then his fingers search for the small amulet he has been secretly carving these last many days. He does not trust his old fingers and turns the pouch upside down, but nothing falls from it. He checks to see if there is a hole, but there is none.

His heart begins to pound inside his chest. What evil spirit has stolen his granddaughter's present? He looks around to see if the demon is nearby. Noisy seabirds swoop above, and some black crows sit on a nearby tree, laughing at him. No, they are not so clever, he thinks. Shuksi'em knows there is no time to begin again, and the small leftover pieces of the special stone are not big enough for his stiff fingers to work. A huge wave of sadness engulfs him. He slowly walks back, trying to retrace the path he took, though he knows it is almost impossible to find such a thing once it has dropped into the sand.

In the evening the clan people are tired but happy. Most are content to go to their sleeping spaces early tonight without the usual evening talks. Shuksi'em is glad that *even the children are too tired for stories. He eases himself down on the fresh bedding, pulls his bearskin up to his chin, and struggles to find a comfortable position, but cannot.*

"Ah, I am so tired that I feel like an empty clamshell," Talusip says as she prepares herself for sleep. "Are you as tired, Husband?"

Shuksi'em has no desire to talk to his wife and pretends to be asleep.

"Why are you not answering, old man? I know you are not sleeping."

Still Shuksi'em does not speak. He is suffering a great loss and wants to do it alone.

"I found something today that should interest you." Talusip senses the deep pain her mate is feeling and stops her teasing. She curls up close and wraps her arm around him.

He feels her tough hands grope for his and then slip a small object into his palm. His fingers close around the familiar little stone. "Where did you find it?" he asks in a low voice.

"Under the old cedar bedding. It was only because I was taking out the old boughs today that I found it."

Shuksi'em's heart is singing. "You are such a good wife," he tells Talusip. He will still have time to finish Sleek Seal's present tomorrow.

"Be more careful with this precious gift. And, of course, did you consider that now every granddaughter will be asking for one?"

Shuksi'em smiles behind the curtain of darkness and tucks the tiny treasure under his deerskin pillow.

When I stumbled into the kitchen the next morning, Uncle Stuart was standing at the stove, whistling and frying eggs. "Morning, sleepyhead. I'm glad you're finally up. Saves me the trouble of coming to wake you. I've made my Saturday morning special — eggs, easy over, with lightly buttered toast and some fresh juice." I looked at the runny mess in the pan and smiled.

"Thanks, Uncle Stuart. Looks delicious." When I sopped up the egg with the bread, it actually tasted pretty good. "Where's Aunt Margaret?"

"She went out a while ago to do a few things. She mentioned you wanted to go up and see your friend at the hospital. Is it okay if I take you?"

"Sure." I looked at the clock on the wall, and immediately became stiff with panic. Eddy would be here any time, and I didn't want to be around when she arrived. "Uncle Stu, could we leave now?"

He grinned. "Right now? Don't you think you should get dressed first?"

"Not a problem. I can be ready in about three minutes."

Uncle Stuart scratched his head and gave me one of those I'll-never-understand-kids looks. "Ah, well, I guess so."

I ran up the stairs two at a time and pulled on the crinkled T-shirt from off the floor and the blue jeans that were still wet around the cuffs. Soon I was downstairs at the front door, jangling the car keys to hurry Uncle Stuart. Just as we drove up Crescent Road, I saw Eddy's red pickup coming down the hill. I shrank into the seat and hoped she hadn't noticed us.

When we reached Mrs. Hobbs's floor, there were some loud, boisterous nurses standing at the desk.

"Oh, sure, the only reason you stayed overtime is

because Jen just brewed a fresh pot of coffee," chortled a chubby nurse. They didn't seem to notice us pass by. When I entered the room, there was the same sad quietness as before. But where was Mrs. Hobbs? I looked at every patient in the room to see if she'd switched beds. Then I ran out to the hall to check the number on the door. It was the right room.

Suddenly, I felt as light as a feather. "She's gone home. She said she'd be fine, so she must have gone home, right?"

"Hmm. Well, maybe she did," Uncle Stuart said. "I'll go and check with the nurses to find out what they know."

I stayed outside the room while he went to the front desk. There were lots of older people in the rooms and halls. Some sat in wheelchairs or shuffled along with the help of walkers. I turned my gaze away — it didn't seem right for me to watch them struggle.

The nurses were still laughing about something until Uncle Stuart interrupted them. I was anxious to find out about Mrs. Hobbs, so I strolled down to the nurses' station.

"I'm very sorry that you weren't informed," said the chubby nurse in a low voice. "But Mrs. Hobbs passed on quite suddenly last night. She was such a lovely person. We all liked her so much. Are you her family?"

I couldn't breathe and started gasping for air. I'd heard what the nurse had said, but she couldn't be telling the truth. I was here. I was here to see Mrs. Hobbs. But when I looked into my uncle's eyes I knew it was true. I stumbled toward the stairwell and fumbled my way down the steps. My uncle called after me, but I began to run.

Once I was outside the hospital, I ran until a stitch in my side forced me to slow to a walk. But even then I kept going until I found myself standing alongside an old railway track. I walked awkwardly along it — at first taking tiny steps for each single tie. But that was too slow, so I stretched my legs to take two at a time. Nervously, I watched and listened for trains as I followed the tracks that led to Crescent Beach.

After I got to Thousand Stairs, I jumped down from the track and went the rest of the way along the shoreline. When I finally arrived at Beecher Street, there were people everywhere. I pulled the hood on my jacket over my head and tied it tight around my face. Even though it made me hot, I wanted to be invisible. Like a ghost hiding behind a shroud of sadness, I watched women pushing buggies, couples holding hands, dogs running for sticks at the water's edge, and kids clambering over logs. The muscles in my throat tightened, and I wanted to yell at them all for being happy, for going on with their lives — without Mrs. Hobbs.

I hurried to Blackie's Spit where I knew there would be hardly anyone. My feet were sore, and I flopped onto the sand. I'd been walking for so long, trying to keep my feelings in check, that now the stillness was like an open door and all the grief came bursting in on me.

Angrily, I scooped up handfuls of sand. After it sifted through my fingers, there were small bits of broken clamshell and a couple of mudflat snails resting in my palms. Shells — they protected the creatures living inside. I needed a shell, one that kept out the feelings, the memories, the guilt. Then I squeezed my eyes tight, making a barrier against the tears.

CHAPTER 10

With everything that had happened in the past two days, the last thing I wanted was to see Eddy. Now that I'd become a grave robber like Mr. Grimbal, something about me had changed, and she was sure to notice. I breathed easier when I came up the street and saw that her old pickup was nowhere around. But I wondered who owned the Mustang convertible parked in the driveway. Quietly, I opened the front door, hoping I could sneak up to my room without anyone noticing.

"Oh, it's Peggy. She's home." Aunt Margaret was in the living room. I almost crumpled to the floor in a heap.

When she came out, she looked at me as if I were a pathetic stray cat standing in her hallway. "You poor thing. I heard the news from Stuart."

"Aunt Margaret, I don't feel like talking. I just want to go to my room."

"Yes, of course. But maybe you could come in here for a moment. There's someone here I think you should meet."

I heaved my chest and followed my aunt into the living room. That was when my heart jumped into my throat again.

"Hello, Peggy," said Eddy, who was sitting on the sofa next to a very long-legged man.

I held my breath and tried to avoid looking into her

eyes. "Hi," I mumbled. Eddy looked tired and sad. She knows, I thought.

"Your aunt just told us about Helen passing on. I didn't realize you both were such good friends. You know she was a good friend of mine, too."

How could I have forgotten about that? "Yes, she told me how much you both loved to spend your summers here in Crescent Beach," I said quietly. I tried to imagine Mrs. Hobbs and Eddy when they were young girls. Mrs. Hobbs would have been sort of elegant, but not in a stuffy way. Eddy was probably ... more like me.

I glanced over at the olive-skinned man. He had black hair streaked with grey and wore a Montreal Canadiens cap. He caught me staring at him. "Hi," he said.

I felt my cheeks flush.

"Oh, I'm sorry, Peggy. This is Chief Donald Lloyd."

The lanky man stood and shook my hand. "I'm very sorry to hear about your loss."

I liked his soft voice and calm face. His features reminded me of the woman in Mrs. Hobbs's book.

"It was Peggy and her uncle who discovered the burial," Eddy said. "And I should add that she's turned out to be one of my best assistants."

My face felt as if it were on fire.

"It must have been quite a shock to find an ancient burial in your backyard, Peggy," the chief said.

My mind flashed back to the day Uncle Stuart and I first found the skull. "I guess it was for my aunt and uncle. But for me, I'd have to say I was more fascinated than shocked."

The chief smiled at me as if he approved of my answer. "And for good reason, too. Eddy was just explaining how much you both have learned about my ancestor."

"Your ancestor?"

"Yes, I'm also Coast Salish like him. Today our people live on the Semiahmoo Reserve, but there was a time when all this land was occupied by only Salish speakers. It was the best place for our ancestors to come for fishing, hunting, and gathering fruit." I remembered that Mr. Grimbal had said something similar. "And as you've discovered, it was also where our dead were buried."

The word *dead* seemed to hang in the air along with a sudden sense of grief and gloom.

My aunt broke the silence by trying to reignite the conversation cheerfully. "It's certainly been a learning opportunity for us all, though Peggy was the one who threw herself into the archaeology and excavation. Isn't that right, Peggy?"

"Yeah, I guess. I never realized it was possible to get to know someone who was …"

"Not alive," my aunt volunteered.

Usually, that sort of thing would have been frustrating, but I sensed Aunt Margaret was trying to help. When I looked at the three faces, it was hers that seemed most eager to hear what I had to say.

"Chief Lloyd, he may have been your ancestor — and I don't mean any disrespect — but you don't know him at all." I made the mistake of looking at Eddy, and my voice got all wobbly. "I've seen the story of his bones. They tell of an old man who lived a long and useful life filled with pain and challenges. His back was stiff and crooked and his hands were gnarled. He couldn't do what the other men in the tribe could, like fishing and hunting, but he found other ways to contribute to his clan. Sometimes he used his teeth to grind and soften the fibres used for basket making. And though he might have been slow, he used his hands to make things. He was a craftsman, a woodworker, maybe even an artist."

My mind could see the tiny carved face. "When he was growing up, he survived a period of near starvation. Then he had a terrible ear infection that caused him to lose his hearing. And as if that wasn't hard enough, he endured a painful and scary skull operation — probably no one he knew had ever seen such a thing. I think someone who had survived stuff like that must have been brave."

The chief nodded in agreement.

"And because he was old, he must have known a lot — the kind of things that could help his people. Like the best places to fish and how to tan hides, or all his clan's history and stories. And when he died, his family had him buried carefully on his side, with all his tools and belongings so he'd be okay in his next life. I think that showed they really cared about him."

Until that moment I hadn't realized that my cheeks were streaked with tears and my heart was numb. That was when I knew Eddy and Mrs. Hobbs weren't the only friends I'd betrayed. "I'm sorry, but I'm not feeling well. I'm going to my room now."

"Of course, this has been a very difficult day for you," Aunt Margaret said. "You go and rest for a while and I'll come and check on you later."

"Before you go," said Chief Lloyd, whose dark eyes were full of thoughts that could never be shared. "When my ancestor was buried here long ago, it was meant to be forever." He spoke gently, with no trace of resentment in his voice. "If somehow he's aware of what's happened, he may feel sad that his earthly remains and burial ground have been disturbed. But he'd also feel your great concern for him. On his behalf, I thank you and Dr. McKay for your care and respect."

As I walked up the stairs, I heard Eddy's voice. "We should have most of the remains removed by tomorrow, Mrs. Randall. Then, once I've made sure we've recovered all the burial goods, we're done." Aunt Margaret must have been happy to hear that.

Then I heard the chief speak in a much softer voice. "Dr. McKay, the band members have given you their permission to study the remains and burial goods. But in time we'd like our ancestor returned so we can give him a resting place on our land."

I closed the door and dropped onto my bed where I finally let everything out. I cried until my brain throbbed and my face was raw. Everything in my life was crap. My mom was thousands of miles away, my aunt thought I was a horrible brat, I was a thief in partnership with Mr. Grimbal, my closest friend was gone — and I never got a chance to show her how much I cared about her. And if that wasn't bad enough, it was only a matter of time before Eddy found out what I'd done and she'd hate me, too. I would've berated myself all night, but after a while I couldn't keep my eyes open and drifted off to sleep.

When I woke, the room was dark and there was such a quiet stillness I knew it was the middle of the night. My stomach started growling, and I realized I'd missed supper. I tiptoed down the stairs and looked in the fridge for something to eat. Duff rubbed up against my leg, and I bent down and scratched him under the chin.

"Sorry for yelling at you yesterday," I whispered. I poured myself a glass of milk and put some in a bowl for him. Then I helped myself to a piece of Aunt Margaret's carrot cake.

I went out and sat on the back porch where the moonlight had cast a soft white glow over everything. Even though I knew the tarp that covered the burial was orange, it looked grey and colourless. Above, the sky was packed with tiny specks of starlight. I thought about what I'd learned in school about astronomy, like how the starlight I was seeing was actually sent out millions of years ago.

That was when it hit me — an epiphany Mom would have said. Lots of things had changed in Crescent Beach over the past three or four thousand years, but not the moon and stars. This was the same star-speckled sky the old man had looked at every night of his life. Then I noticed the slightly pungent smell of seaweed and salt water drifting in on the gentle evening breeze. And there, beyond the houses and trees, was the sound of the waves lapping onto the shore — *whoosh ... whoosh ... whoosh* — like the Earth's rhythmic heartbeat. I realized I was connected ... to the past ... to him ... to Mrs. Hobbs, wherever she was.

After I bathed in this knowledge for some time, I knew I'd tell Eddy about the carved pendant. No matter what she'd think of me, we had to try to get it back.

"Hi, Peggy. How are you feeling?" I'd already jumped off the steps by the time I realized it was only Aunt Margaret. "Oops. Sorry to startle you. I guess you were so deep in thought you didn't hear me."

"That's okay."

Aunt Margaret opened the fridge. "Got room for another piece of carrot cake?"

I nodded. I could always make room for one more slice of her famous carrot cake. She took the cake from the fridge and dished out a piece for us both, then motioned for me to join her at the kitchen table.

"You know, this was my mother's recipe. I used to love helping her in the kitchen. She taught me to cook and bake just about everything." Aunt Margaret picked at the cake on her plate. "At first I loved cooking, because it was something special she and I could do together. Your mom, Stella, and Norma — they hated anything to do with the kitchen — so they were always outside playing, getting dirty, just like you. Then Mom passed on, and all of a sudden I had three little girls to care for, cook for, make decisions for, and I was barely more than a girl myself."

I wasn't sure why Aunt Margaret was telling me all this, so I sat quietly and listened.

"Peggy, I've been thinking about the conversation we had the other day. Well, it was more like an argument. I realize now I've been trying to parent you the way I tried to parent my sisters. I told them when to get up, when to go to bed, what clothes to put on, what to do — everything. I thought that's what a parent did. But you reminded me that it wasn't an effective way to raise children back then, and it's not the way to do it now.

"I see now, Peggy, that I don't need to make you into someone who's responsible, caring, or disciplined. If anything, my job is to support you as you go about discovering your innate goodness." She brushed at her eyes. "When I listened to you talk about the things you've learned from reading those bones, and all the great things Dr. McKay had to say about you, I realized you already are a caring, responsible, and capable girl. So I'm sorry for not realizing that sooner. And I know I'm not your mother, but believe me when I say that I love you, no matter what you wear, or how messy your room gets, or even when we disagree."

Her words embraced me like a long, warm hug. I leaned over and kissed her cheek. "I'm sorry, too, Aunt Margaret. You really aren't as horrible as I made you out to be. Lots of it was my fault, too."

Outside, the first light of dawn was appearing on the horizon, and wispy grey clouds floated across the pink-and-orange sky. Aunt Margaret cleared the dishes from the table and gestured for me to come upstairs. "Do you think we should try to get a few hours of rest before the day really begins?"

I nodded.

After I crawled into bed and Aunt Margaret was closing my bedroom door, I knew there was more that needed to be said. "Aunt Margaret, wait," I whispered. "There's something I need to tell you." She came back and sat on the edge of the bed. There, in the dark, I told her about accidentally finding the carving, about making a deal to sell it to Mr. Grimbal, and even about trying to get it back. I also told her how Mrs. Hobbs felt that artifacts from Crescent Beach belonged in the museum.

"She said the only way people will know what a wonderful past Crescent Beach has is by preserving it for them. And that won't happen unless the people who find the artifacts and remains respect and appreciate Native heritage." I felt a renewed sense of shame as my words hung in the air, but there was also a wave of relief that I'd finally told someone.

Then I sat back and waited. Even after everything she'd said earlier, somehow I still expected Aunt Margaret to be disappointed with me. She didn't say anything for a really long time. I couldn't take the silence. "I guess you think I was pretty stupid, right?"

Still she said nothing. Then, finally, she looked up from her lap and spoke so softly I could barely hear her. "No, Peggy, I don't think you were stupid. You made a big mistake, and it sounds like you already realize that, and even tried to correct it. I'd say that you learned your lesson. But now I have something I need to tell you."

I was so afraid of what she was going to say that my hands started to shake under the bedcovers.

"At first I was anxious to get those bones out of my yard. Besides it being kind of creepy, I felt inconvenienced by the excavation. I allowed Bob Puddifoot to bring Mr. Grimbal to the house, with the belief he could speed things along. There was also some talk of financial compensation, too."

She took a deep breath. "Boy, I'm glad we're talking in the dark ... because I can hardly stand myself. Anyway, I let Mr. Grimbal poke around in the burial to see if there was anything important, anything of value. I made him promise not to move too much. Then he picked up the skull, and that's when he found the pendant.

"I don't know why, but I suddenly felt terrible about letting him touch the burial, even about letting him into our yard. So I made him leave. He was so angry that he actually frightened me. I realize now he was waiting for you to find it, was maybe even spying on you. With all that's been going on between us, I guess it didn't take him long to find you at a weak moment. What happened wasn't your fault. It was mine."

Wow, I hardly knew what to say. In a funny way I was glad to know I wasn't the only one who'd done something stupid. Then I reached out and took Aunt Margaret's hand. "Okay, so we both goofed up. What are we going to do about it?"

Shuksi'em is not well today and cannot leave the clan house. The people are collecting firewood and are preparing spaces for the guests to sleep. Sleek Seal stands gracefully before her grandfather so he can admire her ceremonial shell necklace and her dress made from new deer hide.

"You have done well, Granddaughter. If I did not know better, I would think it was your aunts who made these fine things." The girl's cheeks glow a tender pink, and her smile is one of joy. He motions for her to come closer so he can examine the beautiful design of shells better. "It is good that you have blended your mother's tusk shells with the dentalia from our Nootkan cousins. Like our people, they exist in harmony."

"The secret to the shells' brilliant shine, Grandfather, is to gather them when they are fresh."

"Ah, very clever," Shuksi'em says, pretending to be surprised.

"Mother thinks I have not finished preparing my costume. So you are the first to see me in my finery." The girl grins.

"Why is it you have deceived her, Sleek Seal?"

"It was the only way she would let me stay behind today. The aunts have kept me so busy preparing food for the feast.

They never give me a moment of peace. Everyone knows how important it is that I look my best for the ceremony, so they have given me today to finish." Her smile is like a bright, warm light.

Shuksi'em cannot help himself, and he snickers at this cunning child.

"But since my work is done, what I really want is to hear a story, one that I have never heard before."

"Ah, now I see your true purpose. And since you are so clever, I shall tell you one — a true story about what happens when people are too crafty." Sleek Seal's eyes widen with anticipation. "This story was given to me by my elders when I was a young man and to them from many generations of family storytellers. It tells of a dark time when our clan had not learned the danger of greed and how it is the cause of shame and death. Are you frightened, Sleek Seal? I would not want to scare you." Shuksi'em grins at his granddaughter.

"Oh, Grandfather! I am never afraid when you tell stories. Well, almost never. Go on. I want to hear."

"Well, if you are sure then. It was fall and your ancestors were having a wedding potlatch. It was meant to be a happy time. And as is the custom, many gifts were to be distributed to the guests. The bride's family decided they would scramble the goat-wool robes to the common people. During the game, there was much disorder as people grabbed and pulled at the beautiful coats. Two men were fighting over the same coat — neither generous enough to let go. The struggle ended when the older man slashed the younger one's face with his sharp clamshell knife.

"That night the wife of the younger man thought to take revenge for her husband's humiliation, and she searched *the forest until she caught a frog. When no one was looking, she took some of the other man's tea and a small piece of his sleeping mat and forced them down the frog's throat. Then she sewed up the frog's mouth and attached it to a long rod and planted it in the river's mouth. She meant for the evil thing to be washed away, causing her husband's enemy to choke on this bad luck until death." Shuksi'em stretches his arms and yawns loudly. "Perhaps I should finish the story another time, Sleek Seal."*

"Grandfather, you are teasing me. You know I could not bear for you to stop now. And I am sure I will be haunted if you do not finish the story."

Shuksi'em shakes with laughter until strands of his long grey hair loosen from their braids. Sleek Seal laughs herself at his nearly toothless grin.

"I would never be the cause of your haunting, dear granddaughter, so I will continue as you have asked. When the wife returned to the big house, someone overheard her telling her husband about what she had done. That night, when the older man began to vomit and choke, word of her deed passed quickly through the big house. The clan was angry and afraid that her witchcraft could be so powerful. Soon there was a frenzy and the people began to shout, 'Kill the wicked ones before they kill us.' The couple was taken to the shell mound where they were bound together in an embrace. Many of the men took their sharpest arrows and shot the man and woman until their bodies slumped to the ground. They were buried right where they died, while the clan shaman called on the spirits to cleanse the village of their evil souls."

Shuksi'em pauses to let the details of the story sift deeper into his granddaughter's mind. He watches as she considers these events. Only a few such stories of war and violence have passed down through time. His people are peaceful, and he has never known such strange happenings in his own lifetime.

"Did the older man die, Grandfather?" Sleek Seal asks.

Shuksi'em smiles at her question. "No, Granddaughter. In the morning, when he felt better, he told his wife that he had eaten too many of the clams during the feast. One had some fine pieces of shell that lodged in his throat, causing him irritation. Then, when he had heard what had happened the night before, he collapsed on the spot and died of shock."

"The life lesson is clear to me, Grandfather. First, had the two men found a fair and generous solution to the problem with the goat-wool robe, the matter would have ended peacefully. If the wife had used more sense and less craftiness, she would not have caused such alarm among the clan people. And finally, the ancestors were too hasty in their judgment. If they had waited, they would have seen that the older man was not harmed. Our people must never forget this story, Grandfather. It is good that you have told me."

Shuksi'em strokes the girl's head, silently approving her wisdom. Then he pulls his small deerskin pouch out from under his bed and unties the string. "Sleek Seal, I have something I want to give you." He removes the small amulet and gives it a last few rubs until the little round face gleams. The pendant hangs from a thin piece of bear-gut string. "I have carved this charm from a rare stone brought by the traders. It has been blessed by the shaman and will give you courage when you go to your new clan. The goodness in your heart will only make it more powerful, so keep it close." He wants to say more, to tell her she will be missed, but the sting in his eyes makes him turn away.

Sleek Seal admires the stone. She has never seen such a charm as this, and she knows how hard it has been for her grandfather to carve such details. Her heart feels hot in her chest and is nearly bursting.

CHAPTER 11

Aunt Margaret and I decided that telling Eddy was the first step in trying to fix this mess. By the time her pickup pulled up to the house, my stomach was in such a tight ball that I could hardly stand up. Then, when I saw Chief Lloyd drive up and park his Mustang behind Eddy's truck, my heart sank.

Aunt Margaret noticed the chief, too, and sighed deeply. "All right, Peggy, this is going to be tough, but we'll do it together." She marched over to the front door and opened it wide. "Good morning, Dr. McKay and Chief Lloyd."

"Hello, Mrs. Randall," Eddy said. "Today is an important one, and the chief wanted to be here to offer a prayer and observe the final removal of the burial. Is Peggy feeling up to participating?"

"Ah, well there's something she and I need to talk to you about. Would you both be kind enough to come into the house?"

New waves of panic wrenched at my stomach. It was bad enough to have to confess to Eddy. Why did she have to invite the chief, too?

After they were both seated in the living room, my aunt began telling our story. "When we first discovered the remains in our backyard, I was pretty disturbed. You could even say I was horrified. I now regret feeling that way."

Eddy smiled. "Actually, Mrs. Randall, your response wasn't all that unusual."

"Well, maybe not … but there are some things you need to know."

As Aunt Margaret explained everything that had happened, the happy expression melted off Eddy's face and her normally warm eyes turned dark. It was harder to get a reading on the chief. His calm demeanour didn't change at all.

Even though I felt like barfing up breakfast, I was also overcome with appreciation for my aunt. I could never have done this alone. She seemed so calm and cool as she took most of the blame, including the part when I sold the carving to Mr. Grimbal. After she finished, there was a long silence. I stared hard at the floor, afraid to look up and catch Eddy's eye.

"I see" was all Eddy said. I expected to hear how disgusted she was … maybe some yelling or even stomping. But I wasn't prepared for silence. Then, after several minutes, it was Chief Lloyd who spoke first, breaking the tension.

"You think your story is a new one? Such things have been happening for a very long time." He gazed out the window as he spoke. "Since the first white land agent showed up over a hundred and twenty years ago and claimed this place for the Dominion of Canada, Salish people have seen their land diminished and their culture reduced to collectibles for the curious." His tone wasn't sad or critical, just matter-of-fact. "But not everyone wants to see the ancient remains and possessions turned into bookshelf ornaments." He glanced over at Eddy.

"That's right, Chief," Eddy said. "Not everyone is like Walter Grimbal."

"Or me," I added, feeling the need to take responsibility for what I'd done.

"No, Peggy, you don't fit into that category," the chief said. "No one who speaks so eloquently about my ancestor as you did yesterday could feel that way."

The first knot in my stomach came undone.

"Chief Lloyd's right, Peggy," Eddy said. "I don't excuse what you did, but given all the circumstances, I'd say your actions were misguided, not motivated by greed or disrespect. And, Mrs. Randall, I appreciate your honesty in coming forward with this."

The next knot in my intestines unwound, and the feeling returned to my fingers when I finally relaxed my white knuckles.

"Peggy and I just want to do what we can to fix all this." Aunt Margaret seemed as relieved as I was that everything was finally out in the open.

"Well, fixing all this really comes down to fixing Walter Grimbal." Eddy's eyes were now distant as if she were remembering something from long ago. "You might find it hard to believe, but there was a time when Walter was one of the fiercest advocates for preserving prehistoric cultural remains. His wife, Lily, and he first moved to Crescent Beach in the late 1950s. At that time there were few people who lived here year-round. It didn't take them long to start finding arrowheads, bone and stone tools, and even human remains. Back then many artifacts lay right on the surface. Other times they turned up in a vegetable garden or when digging a hole to bury a family pet. At the time there was no Heritage

Conservation Branch, no local museum, and people didn't see a reason for being concerned about all these strange remnants of the past.

"But Lily and Walter were fascinated by them. They kept every artifact they found and eventually built up quite a collection. There were a few others, including me, who realized the importance of these artifacts. When the Grimbals opened the Real Treasures and Gifts shop, they devoted an entire corner of the store to the display of artifacts and photos of the local Native culture. None of it was for sale, though they got lots of offers. Eventually, we were able to build a museum. When it first opened, the largest part of the collection was Coast Salish artifacts donated by Lily and Walter."

"I can't believe we're talking about the same Mr. Grimbal," I said. "What made him change?"

"Lily and Walter had a son, Thomas. He was born with Down's syndrome. The kid was sweet, but because of his mental disability he was never able to look after himself. Lily usually doted on him. But one day she left him briefly to make a trip to the gift store — by this time he was well into his twenties. I guess he decided to go to the beach. He'd never learned to swim, but he always loved the water. By the time she and Walter found his things on the shore, it was too late. The boy's body was found two days later, washed up on the mud flats of Point Roberts ..." Eddy's voice trailed off.

"That's really sad," I said. "So you're saying that's what made him change?"

"No. It was what made Lily change. She became distant from everyone and just seemed to drop out of life. She wasn't interested in anything — not in the museum or the store, not even in her husband. One day Walter came home to find her body slumped by the gas stove."

That was a lot of sorrow to take in, and I didn't need Eddy to spell out the rest of the story. I think a lot of people would've crawled into a hole, like Mr. Grimbal, and just stopped caring.

"Over the years the shop has gone downhill," Eddy continued, "and so has Walter Grimbal. I tried to ignore him as well as I could, but now he's gone too far. He's got to be stopped, Peggy. From what you've told me, he may have already sold the carved artifact. The only thing left to do is bring in the police." She pulled out her cell phone from one of the pockets on her fisherman's vest.

"The Heritage Conservation Act permits only a qualified field director — that's me — to remove or examine any artifacts or remains from a site. In other words, Walter had no business messing with the burial, even if you invited him, Mrs. Randall. Now the most I could do would be to slap him on the wrist with a fine. So that's why you need to press charges against him for trespassing and coercing a minor to break the law. Peggy, you'll have to be willing to be a witness."

At that moment I wished this was the Friday night late movie and I could shut off the TV and go to bed. Exhaustion had crept back into every muscle, blood vessel, and bone in my body. But as I watched Eddy press the pads on her cell phone, I shot off the sofa with some hidden reserve of energy.

"Eddy, wait. I know you might find it hard to trust me right now, but I want you to give me a chance to fix this my way."

She didn't look too convinced. "Peggy, I've tried

many times over the years to get through to Walter."

"Look, there was a time when I didn't feel anything for the old man buried in our yard. But then you showed me I could know him — in part — if I took the time to look closely. If I can do that for someone who lived thousands of years ago, maybe there's a chance I can do that with Mr. Grimbal, too. Just give me an hour."

After a few moments, Eddy's frown dissolved and her face relaxed. "Okay, you've got one hour. That's how long it will take us to finish removing the burial. But after that …"

"I know. Thanks, Eddy." I took off down the street at a jog. I didn't have some amazing plan. I just wanted to try talking to Mr. Grimbal, to get him to give me back the ancient pendant.

After I got to his store, I gasped out loud when I saw the CLOSED sign on the door. When I started banging on the window, I got odd looks from people passing by on the sidewalk. Then I tried the door and was surprised when it flung open. I stepped inside and got that familiar shiver as I passed Tsonokwa.

"What do you want now, kid? I told you already that our deal's done. Finished. Over."

For the first time I wondered if the deep and furrowed creases on his forehead and at the corners of his mouth were really from being an angry curmudgeon, or just from being sad and lonely. I noticed his shoulders were stooped and that his fingers were gnarled. And he had no laugh lines around his eyes like Mrs. Hobbs's. Still, I gazed carefully into them to see if there was something I could recognize.

"I just want to talk, Mr. Grimbal." I hoped he hadn't

noticed that my hands were shaking.

"I only have time to talk business," he snapped. "And unless you've come here to do business, I'm not interested in talking."

Desperately, I tried to think of something clever to say, but in the end I just opened my mouth and words tumbled out. "You pretend you don't care about protecting Crescent Beach's prehistory, but I don't believe that's true."

"Oh, I'm not pretending. I really don't care." He waved at all the artifacts in the store. "All these things are just junk from the past — stuff to clutter up shelves and collect dust. And I'll tell you something, nobody else really cares, either, about the prehistory of Crescent Beach, about dead cultures and dead men. They'll never understand that their pretty little beachside homes, gardens, and lives are only one more, tiny stratigraphic layer in a deep midden of human experience."

For some reason, at that moment I remembered something Mrs. Hobbs had said. She was quoting a writer named Ralph Waldo Emerson. At the time I was more interested in how a guy with such a dorky name like Ralph Waldo could possibly write anything that would be relevant to me. But the line kind of stuck in my mind. Actually, it was a question: "Why do we grope among the dry bones of the past?" And just as suddenly I thought I knew the answer to Mr. Emerson's question.

"Mr. Grimbal, you're right. There are a lot of people who don't care. But I do. And so does Eddy and my aunt. And so did Mrs. Hobbs. And if we look really hard, I'll bet there are others, too." My face got hot when he sneered and laughed callously. I tried to ignore him and went on. "I think it takes courage to look at the past. A lot of times the things we find are scary, or make us sad, or just remind us that we won't live forever. But if we don't look back, then we'll lose all the good things and the lessons the ancients can teach us."

I remembered the look on his face when he first held the tiny carving. "You care, too, Mr. Grimbal. I saw it on your face the day I brought you the stone."

Mr. Grimbal glared through narrowed eyes. "Ha. The only thing you saw when I held that scratched-up rock were fat old dollar signs in my eyes. So if you think you can sweet-talk me into giving you back that artifact, you can forget it. Now get out of here and quit wasting my time."

"Okay, I'll go. But there's something I want to ask you first. If all this stuff is just worthless junk, why do you keep it? Why don't you actually sell any of these ancient Native artifacts?"

"What? Of course, I sell this stuff. What do you think I am … nuts? I'm running a business."

"I'll tell you what I think, Mr. Grimbal. All of these things aren't just pieces of the ancient past. They're part of your past … and Lily's."

He waved my words off as if they were annoying black flies.

"Mr. Grimbal, what do you think your wife would want you to do? Would she want these important pieces of pre-history tucked away on your shelves for only you to enjoy? Or would she want everyone to have the chance to learn from the past, to know what you know?" For a moment I thought I saw the hardness crumble and something soften in his eyes. But just as quickly his face stiffened again.

"Okay, kid, you gave it your best shot. Now it's time to get lost." He nudged me the last few steps out the door and bolted the lock.

Mr. Grimbal was right. I had given it my best shot, and it failed … again.

For some time now Shuksi'em has been unable to leave his bed. Sleek Seal sits next to him feeding him fresh deer meat she has chewed into soft, tiny morsels. He is sorry the illness kept him from enjoying the celebration. The visitors have left the big house now, and Shuksi'em is glad that his granddaughter did not go with them. He thinks her father made a wise decision to give her another season with her own clan. But the union with Hulutin next year will be good for making bonds between the coast people. The clan is happy because the young man's parents left many gifts of wealth to secure the marriage between the two young people.

Shuksi'em knows his life is near its end, but he must not speak of it. It angers his wife, who says, "You cannot die, you foolish old man. I need your help next spring to make my basket string."

His face breaks into a toothless grin, his pink gums lit by firelight. "No, it is you who is foolish, my dear wife. How can I chew your cattail or roots when I have no teeth left? And my hands are more knotted than your string."

That night Talusip wraps her full, warm body around her husband's. She is afraid an evil spirit is waiting nearby to take him away. If she wills it, she can keep him safe for another night. But soon Shuksi'em's low, heavy breathing and the exhaustion of her own sadness lulls her to sleep.

Embraced in his wife's arms, Shuksi'em feels content and warm. Her large body eases the pain from his own.

Closing his eyes, he thinks of his life. Yes, he has had his share of trouble, but it has been a good life. Then he whispers, "Come, Great Spirit, I am ready to go."

CHAPTER 12

Life's curveballs — that was what I was thinking about when this whole thing began. How sometimes they beaned you on the head ... and sometimes they ended up okay. But that day in the Real Treasures and Gifts store I'd gotten one right between the eyes. Maybe I'd discovered something about reading bones, but I still had a lot to learn about reading people. I wanted to fix everything, but instead I had a lifetime to relive my biggest mistake over and over.

After Mr. Grimbal pushed me out the door, I didn't have the courage to go back and face Eddy again. Instead I walked to the beach. When I got there, I took off my shoes, waded up to my knees in the cool, clear water, and squished the sand between my toes. All around me was a swirl of activity — a black lab galloping into the water after a tennis ball, kids decorating their sandcastle with bits of white clamshells, and sailboats making their way back and forth across the bay. It all reminded me of Mrs. Hobbs, and even though I tried really hard to stop it, my chest heaved and my eyes filled with tears. I remembered what Mrs. Hobbs had said about having a good cry, so I let it all out until I was as empty as the little boy's sand pail.

When I finally headed for home, it was nearly suppertime. I wondered if there would be a police car waiting out front, but there was only Eddy's truck. I scowled to myself but knew there was no point trying to avoid her. When I came into the yard, I noticed a wooden box a little bigger than a briefcase. Inside were all the bones from the burial, carefully wrapped in foam and tucked neatly side by side. Chief Lloyd was gone, but Eddy was still working in the pit that now appeared strangely bare. She must have been deep in thought, because she didn't notice me. I cleared my throat to get her attention.

"Um, you were right, Eddy. Nothing I said got through to him."

"Who? Oh, you mean Walter?"

"Of course, I mean Walter. Who else would I be talking about? He wouldn't listen to anything I said."

"Hmm, is that so?"

Was this her way of rubbing it in? "I know it won't help or anything, but I am really sorry."

"Okay."

Okay? Was that all she was going to say. I deserved more. She should get mad, even lecture me the way Aunt Margaret always did. "Eddy, don't you get it? You were right and I was wrong."

"Oh, were you?" Her voice almost sounded playful, though she didn't even look up at me. "I want to dig down another ten centimetres or so just to make sure we got everything. Want to screen a few buckets for me?"

I sighed heavily. I still felt terrible, but it was obvious Eddy wasn't going to talk about it. "Yeah, I guess so." I picked up the pail sitting next to the burial pit and took it over to the screening station. Hoisting it easily, I emptied the contents. I was just about to begin shaking the screen back and forth when I noticed a lump in the dirt. After I picked it up and brushed away the black matrix, I realized it was a small leather pouch.

I had no idea what was inside, but I was pretty sure Eddy had stuck it in the pail for me to discover. When I glanced over at her, she had her nose deep in the pit again and was pretending not to notice me. I untied the string so I could pour out the contents, then gasped when I saw the tiny face tumble into my hand.

"How did you get it?" I barely whispered. When Eddy didn't answer, I felt inside the pouch and pulled out a small piece of paper. It was one of Mr. Grimbal's business cards. Beside the store's name he had handwritten a few words: "Real Treasures and Gifts don't come in boxes." On the back was a note:

> My Lily would have liked you, kid. She had lots of spunk, too. When you're done helping Dr. Know-It-All, maybe there's a thing or two I can teach you. And just because I've gone a little soft in the head, don't think I've forgotten about my three thousand bucks!
>
> — Mr. G

As the tiny black face gleamed up at me, I heard Eddy laugh. Then *bam!* I knew I'd hit that curveball right out of the park.

The men now cover Shuksi'em with a blanket of broken shells, sand, and seaweed. Here his body will stay a short distance from his village ... the shores where he netted fish ... and the forest where he once hunted.

Q'am takes his mother's arm and leads her back toward the clan house. Talusip is weak with sorrow and finds the walk difficult. Her legs feel as if she has a large stone tied to each ankle. They lead the way as the villagers follow.

Back inside the clan house there is a sombre silence as the clan members go about their business. Q'am's wife brings Talusip a cup of hot spruce tea and gently places her arms around the whimpering old woman.

Out on the shell mound Sleek Seal is glad that the others have left. She wants to be alone at her grandfather's side. The tears roll freely down her cheeks. Shuksi'em told her not long ago that he would soon leave this world. "When you go, Grandfather, I will go with you."

He smiled at her and laughed. "No, my child, you will stay here until the Great Spirit calls you to the next place. And when you arrive, I will celebrate just as I did the day you were born."

Now Sleek Seal pulls out her small pendant from under her deerskin cover and removes it over her head. The small, delicate face that Shuksi'em carved was to watch over her as she journeyed through this world. But now she calls on its powers to guard another and pushes it into the soft shell mound that embraces Shuksi'em's body.

"Grandfather, I have the wisdom of your words to guide me in life. But you are going to a strange place. Take this amulet on your journey to keep you safe and to remember me. When we come together again, I will wear it once more." She pushes it even deeper into the mix of broken shells that now envelopes her grandfather — down as far as it will go.

About a week after the excavation was finished my mom

phoned. "So how's my junior archaeologist doing? After finding a prehistoric Indian in Aunt Margie's yard, I hope you're not going to tell me you're now out digging for dinosaurs." Mom laughed as if it was the funniest joke in the world. It was good to hear her so happy.

"Actually, Uncle Stuart says that's it for backyard digging," I said. "Now that we've finished making the pond, he says there's going to be no digging up of anything — not even weeds." Then, before Mom had a chance to crack any more jokes, I poured out the whole story to her — about the fight with Aunt Margaret, about Mrs. Hobbs dying, the pendant ... everything.

When there was silence, I thought maybe I'd made her cry again. "Oh, Peggy, I'm sorry I haven't been there for you."

"Mom, everything's okay. I'm okay. But I still miss you."

"And I miss you, too, Peggy. But I have good news. I've got a job!" At first I felt happy, but then I realized my mom's news meant I'd have to leave Crescent Beach.

"When am I moving with you to Toronto?"

"You're not."

I stopped breathing. "You mean I'm staying here with Aunt Margaret and Uncle Stuart?"

"Yes. For a while ..." After a moment, she added, "And so am I!"

I was confused and didn't know what to say.

"Peggy, my new job is in Vancouver. I'm coming home, sweetheart. We're going to be together in just a few days."

I started to sniffle. "Mom ... that's the best news I've heard in a long time!" My voice had gone up an entire octave so that I sounded like Mickey Mouse.

Later that afternoon I sat by the new pond in the backyard. I liked the way the ferns dipped just over the edge, their graceful fronds reflected in the water. Kneeling, I searched for the baby koi fish swiftly manoeuvring around the rocks and lily pads. I smiled when I looked at the tiny brass plaque Aunt Margaret had made that read: PEGGY'S POND. When I gazed into the clear, dark water, I caught my own happy reflection and laughed. Then I remembered it was time to get ready — TB and I were going sailing.

AUTHOR'S NOTE

While I was learning to be an archaeologist, I had the opportunity to study the remains of an individual removed from a disturbed burial site at Crescent Beach, British Columbia. When I first encountered the remains, housed in the osteology lab at Simon Fraser University, I was fascinated by the bean-shaped hole in the frontal bone and the bent and fused vertebrae that looked more like a boomerang. At first those bones were nothing other than dry and brittle fragments of matter — no more full of life than a bunch of LEGO blocks. But as I learned to read the bones I was surprised to find myself thinking more of the individual they represented and the life he had led. After three months, I completed a detailed analysis and research report, which had grown to be more than a hundred pages. I also had a new-found respect and sense of connection to the individual. This story grew out of that experience.

While all of the characters in this book are fictitious, the town of Crescent Beach does exist on top of a prehistoric Coast Salish summer village and burial site. Problems first began in the early twentieth century when people saw the place as a wonderful summer retreat. As roads and a railway were built, there were major disturbances, and several burial sites were exposed. Some of those sites were simple, like the one described in this book. Later burials were more elaborate and contained such grave goods as beaded bracelets and carved antler handles. Archaeologists believe the height of occupation for the Crescent Beach site was between thirty-four hundred and sixteen hundred years ago.

SELECTED READING

Blanshard, Rebecca, and Nancy Davenport.
    Contemporary Coast Salish Art. Seattle: Stonington
    Gallery, 2005.

Dig: The Archaeology Magazine for Kids. Peterborough,
    NH: Cobblestone Publishing at *www.digonsite.com*.

Francis, Daniel. *Discovering First Peoples and First
    Contacts*. Don Mills, ON: Oxford University Press,
    2000.

Hoyt-Goldsmith, Diane. *Potlatch: A Tsimshian
    Celebration*. New York: Holiday House, 1997.

Panchyk, Richard. *Archaeology for Kids: Uncovering the
    Mysteries of Our Past*. Chicago: Chicago Review
    Press, 2001.

Silvey, Diane. *Spirit Quest*. Toronto: The Dundurn
    Group, second edition, 2008.

Silvey, Diane. *Time of the Thunderbird*. Toronto: The
    Dundurn Group, 2008.

Silvey, Diane, and Diana Mumford. *From Time
    Immemorial: The First People of the Pacific
    Northwest Coast*. Gabriola Island, BC: Pacific Edge
    Publishing, 1999.

Stein, Julie K. *Exploring Coast Salish Prehistory*. Seattle:
    University of Washington Press, 2000.

White, Ellen. *Kwulasulwut: Stories from the Coast
    Salish*. Penticton, BC: Theytus Books, 1981.

_____. *Kwulasulwut II: More Stories from the Coast Salish*. Penticton, BC: Theytus Books, 1997.

White, John R. *Hands-On Archaeology: Real-Life Activities for Kids*. Austin, TX: Prufrock Press, 2005.